Pirates!

I topped the last hill before the shore and caught sight of Joe winding down the lakeshore path. He was ahead, but not by much. As I gunned the throttle, he reached the spot where the two paths met. Then suddenly he braked to a stop.

He gazed out over the bay and I heard his voice on the headset.

"Pirates!" he said. "No way!"

I skidded to a halt beside him.

Sure enough, a huge, old-fashioned pirate ship was sailing across Barmet Bay toward town. A skull-and-crossbones flag flew from its topmost mast, and swarms of pirates in old-fashioned clothing roamed the decks.

Both Joe and I were amazed.

But we were even more amazed as the ship's cannons started firing—right at us!

THE HARDY BOYS

UNDERCOVER BROTHERS®

#1 *Extreme Danger*
#2 *Running on Fumes*
#3 *Boardwalk Bust*
#4 *Thrill Ride*
#5 *Rocky Road*
#6 *Burned*
#7 *Operation: Survival*
#8 *Top Ten Ways to Die*
#9 *Martial Law*
#10 *Blown Away*
#11 *Hurricane Joe*
#12 *Trouble in Paradise*
#13 *The Mummy's Curse*
#14 *Hazed*
#15 *Death and Diamonds*
#16 *Bayport Buccaneers*

Available from Simon & Schuster

THE HARDY BOYS

UNDERCOVER BROTHERS®

#16 Bayport Buccaneers

FRANKLIN W. DIXON

Aladdin Paperbacks
New York London Toronto Sydney

This book is a work of fiction. Any references to historical events, real people, or real locales are used fictitiously. Other names, characters, places, and incidents are the product of the author's imagination, and any resemblance to actual events or locales or persons, living or dead, is entirely coincidental.

ALADDIN PAPERBACKS
An imprint of Simon & Schuster
Children's Publishing Division
1230 Avenue of the Americas
New York, NY 10020

Designed by Lisa Vega
The text of this book was set in Aldine 401 BT.
Manufactured in the United States of America
First Aladdin Paperbacks edition June 2007
10 9 8 7 6 5 4

Library of Congress Control Number 2006937858
ISBN-13: 978-1-4169-3403-5
ISBN-10: 1-4169-3403-0

TABLE OF CONTENTS

Bayport Buccaneers

FRANK

1
A Thief by Any Other Name

"Gun it, Frank! He's getting away!" Joe said.

"Tell me something I don't already know!" I replied.

My brother Joe was right. If we didn't do something fast, Jules Kendallson, the motorcycle bandit, would give us the slip—again.

Joe and I opened up the throttles on our custom bikes and roared after Kendallson. The Northside Woods whizzed past. We ducked branches and darted around the tree trunks blocking the overgrown trail. Every twist and turn presented a new danger—a new place to wipe out.

Kendallson didn't care. He was an expert rider and could have done well on the motocross circuit. Instead he'd turned to crime—stealing bikes instead of racing them. It was up to Joe and me to catch him.

"Frank, low branch!" Joe's voice blared loud and clear over the two-way radio in my helmet.

As I ducked, the tree branch scraped the top of my helmet. Without it, I'd have gotten a nice set of scratches. But if Joe hadn't warned me, I might have lost my head.

"Keep your mind on the trail, big brain!" Joe chided.

My face went red, partly because of what Joe said and partly because I knew he was right. My brother's weakness was that he charged in without thinking; mine was that I sometimes thought *too* much.

"Worrywart!" I called back. "Just stay with him!"

Both Joe and the bandit were ahead of me now. Kendallson twisted his bike around a sharp turn and launched into the air, over a shallow ravine.

Joe skidded in the turn and didn't get as good a jump. He landed hard just below the ravine's rim and lost valuable time as he motored up to the top. I hit the jump better and landed in front of him. I grinned. Sometimes it pays to be the more cautious, older brother.

"Man, that guy is good," Joe said as he roared up behind me.

"If he wasn't, he wouldn't have eluded the cops for so long after busting out of jail," I replied.

"Let's hope they throw away the key this time," Joe said.

"They will, once we catch him," I added, trying to sound more confident than I felt. Kendallson had slipped away from us twice before. Plus he was definitely the better biker. Fortunately Joe and I had been riding the woods north of Bayport since we were kids. We knew these woods better than the crook.

"I'm going to motor around to the left," Joe called over the headset, "and try to cut him off by Benson Ravine."

"Check," I replied. "I'll herd him in that direction." I angled to the right and accelerated again, jumping over the low hills like they were whoop-de-doos at a motocross track. Joe cut in the opposite direction, with the bandit riding between us about fifty yards ahead.

The trees zipped past as I easily swerved and bobbed through the familiar terrain. I was catching up to the bandit. Now I just needed to force Kendallson south so Joe could catch him at the ravine.

Benson Ravine is a wide streambed that cuts through the middle of the wooded hills north of

Bayport. The stream rambles through the forest before eventually emptying into Barmet Bay. There's only one easy way over the ravine, which makes that crossing an ideal trap.

Kendallson spotted me as I angled in on him from the west. He turned east, just like I hoped he would. He wove between the trees ahead of me, keeping dangerously close to the trunks. He clearly wanted me to crash into one, but I knew the area too well for that. Besides, I'd learned my lesson with the tree branch earlier.

I couldn't see Joe through the forest ahead of us, and I hoped the bandit couldn't see him either. With a little luck, Joe would reach the crossing first.

Kendallson glanced back at me as he rode. Little by little I was catching up, and he knew it.

Suddenly he ripped off his helmet and threw it at me.

Now *that* was a stupid thing to do!

The helmet bounced off the forest floor once, and then skipped toward my front tire. I swerved around it and looked up just in time to see a big tree trunk zooming toward my face.

I turned hard, nearly laying the bike on the ground. My back tire kicked up a cloud of dirt and pine needles. I barely missed the tree in front of me and came close to another on my right.

I kicked myself upright again and zoomed after the bandit. He was heading toward the ravine, just as Joe and I had planned. I was blocking his way upstream, so he headed downstream, toward a big old tree trunk that had fallen across the gully. The trunk was like a natural bridge, and it was the only way across the ravine and the rushing stream below.

Kendallson gunned his stolen motorcycle straight for the fallen tree. I looked for Joe and spotted him just before the bandit did. Both of them were heading for the trunk, and it was anyone's guess who would reach the old log first. I knew they'd both get there before me. That was okay, though. I'd done my job. I just hoped Joe would be able to do his.

Unfortunately Kendallson got there first.

He swerved to the right, nearly coming to a stop, and then planted his front tire on the rotting wood. The trunk was wide, but not entirely flat. Staying on it would be a trick, even for a rider as good as Kendallson. He positioned his bike carefully and then began riding across.

Joe skidded to a stop and angled his bike to go over the tree after the bandit. "Don't do it, Joe!" I called over the headset. "The vibration from two bikes at once could bring the whole trunk down!"

Joe looked at me and smiled. "Just what I was thinking," he said. He whipped his bike sideways, put the back tire against the tree trunk, and gunned the engine.

The back tire spun and screeched, kicking clouds of dust and soggy splinters into the air. The tree trunk started vibrating like mad as Kendallson crossed.

The crook's bike wobbled, and before he could do anything about it, he toppled off the log into the rushing stream below. Lucky for him, the stream was wide and pretty deep at that point. He hit the water with a crash and quickly bobbed to the surface; the stolen bike didn't come with him. Kendallson looked dazed. He floundered around helplessly as he drifted downstream toward the bay.

I grinned and shook my head. "He should have kept his helmet on," I said.

Joe nodded. "Safety first," he agreed.

I laughed, but not for the reason Joe thought. It was ironic, him talking about safety; that kind of thing seldom entered my younger brother's mind.

"Come on," I said, "we'll pick up Kendallson downstream and come back for the bike later."

"I'll take the far side, in case he swims across," Joe said. He gunned his engine and zoomed at top speed over the log. It vibrated like it was on the verge of tumbling down, but Joe made it across without even noticing.

I shook my head and followed Kendallson. Like I said, safety was not high on my brother's list of priorities.

We followed the bandit as he floated downstream. Kendallson didn't seem to have any intention of climbing out. I guess the fall took more out of him than I'd thought. He floated with the current, looking dazed. For a moment I thought Joe or I might have to dive into the river and pull him out.

Then I noticed a police boat, out on the bay near the mouth of the stream. The cops aboard spotted Kendallson drifting toward them and headed the boat over to pick him up.

Score!

Joe and I stopped our bikes before we reached the edge of the woods. Even though we're deputized law officers, American Teens Against Crime (ATAC for short) works in secret, so we wanted to avoid getting tangled up with the police.

"The cops will handle Kendallson," said Joe. "I'm sure they'll fish his stolen bike out of the stream too—especially if we give them an anonymous tip where to find it."

"Lucky thing that patrol boat happened by," I said, "or one of us would have had to go swimming. I wonder why the boat's here, though. They don't run a lot of patrols out along the park shore."

"Who cares?" Joe said. "They're here, we're done. Mission accomplished." We both grinned. It always felt good to complete an assignment.

"Let's get home," I said. "Maybe we can catch the arrest on the evening news."

"Race ya," said Joe.

"No fair!" I called. "You're already on the south side of the ravine!"

Joe merely laughed and gunned his engine. I put my bike into high gear, raced back upstream, and zoomed over the rickety log bridge.

Even though Joe had a good head start, he still needed to cut back in my direction to hit Bayshore Drive, the road that runs along the north shore into town.

Joe would be sticking to the trail by the lakeside, but I knew a shortcut. With luck, I could catch up to him before he hit the main road.

I zipped through the woods, dodging low branches and jumping over the bumps in the trail.

I couldn't hear Joe's motorcycle over the roar of my own engine, and he wasn't talking to me on the headset.

Was he ahead of me, or would I actually beat him to the road?

I topped the last hill before the shore and caught sight of Joe winding down the lakeshore path. He was ahead, but not by much. As I gunned the throttle, he reached the spot where the two paths met. Then suddenly he braked to a stop.

He gazed out over the bay and I heard his voice on the headset.

"Pirates!" he said. "No way!"

I skidded to a halt beside him.

Sure enough, a huge, old-fashioned pirate ship was sailing across Barmet Bay toward town. A skull-and-crossbones flag flew from its topmost mast, and swarms of pirates in old-fashioned clothing roamed the decks.

Both Joe and I were amazed.

But we were even more amazed as the ship's cannons started firing—right at us!

JOE

2.
Blowed Up Real Good

"Joe, hit the deck!"

Frank nearly burst my eardrums as he yelled into my headset.

Hit the deck when you're being shot at. No, duh! My brother can be really obvious sometimes. My motorcycle and I were already hugging the ground.

The cannonball—or whatever it was the ship was shooting—blazed over our heads and crashed into the woods right behind us. The ground shook, and a huge puff of smoke billowed into the air. A cheer broke out from the pirate ship. I didn't know who these guys were, but apparently they didn't like the brothers Hardy.

The cannon blazed again.

"Get going!" Frank said, again stating the obvious.

We scrambled forward as quickly as we could, half pushing our bikes, half dragging them, while still keeping our heads low. As we went, Frank kept his eyes glued to the old galleon.

"Less watching, more moving," I said as Frank stepped in front of me. My older brother can be like that sometimes—well, a lot of the time, actually. He analyzes things to death when what's really needed is some solid action.

By the time the pirates blasted their third shot, we'd ducked into the forest and out of the line of fire.

Frank peered through the trees at the ship. "I don't think they're shooting at us," he said.

"Not *now*, they're not," I said. "We're out of range."

"I doubt that," Frank said. "Those weren't real cannonballs they were shooting, anyway. It was just a blast of fire—some type of malfunction, maybe."

"Cannonball or fireball, what does it matter?" I asked. "You're just as dead if one hits you."

"Maybe," said Frank. "But for the most part, the shots seemed to have more flash than bang."

"Well, while you dope out the special effects,

I'll go warn the town," I said. Before Frank could react, I took off down the trail, heading for Bayshore Drive. Frank gunned his motorcycle after me.

"You know, we could just call ahead on our cell phones if we stopped," he said over my headset.

"Where's the fun in that?" I called back.

By the time I hit the pavement, Frank had nearly caught up to me again. I watched in my side mirror as he angled for a small hill. He launched his bike into the air and came down on the blacktop right beside me.

"Bro!" I said, surprised. "That was pretty reckless—for you."

"You're not the only daredevil in this family," he replied.

I didn't mention that I'd seen him checking the traffic in both directions before pulling his stunt. My brother Frank: cautious even when he's daring.

"Stick to the speed limit now that we're on a real road," he said.

"Hey, we need to warn the town," I replied.

"The town probably already knows," Frank said. "The ship's kind of hard to miss—especially with cannons blazing. Besides, Officer Sullivan gave both of us warnings last month—and a speeding ticket would be a rotten way to end a successful mission."

"Hey, we could get ATAC to fix it for us," I said. "We were on a mission when we got those warnings in the first place."

"Maybe ATAC could take care of the ticket," said Frank, "but could they fix the hot water we'd be in with Mom and Aunt Trudy?"

He had me there. Though our dad is one of the founders of ATAC, Mom and Aunt Trudy don't know about the organization—and we can't tell them. (What would be the point of having a secret crime-fighting league if everyone knew about it?)

"Okay," I said, "so I'll stick to the speed limit, even though we could warn the town faster if we didn't."

"We could warn the town faster if we stopped and used our cell phones," Frank repeated.

Sure, he had a point, but there was no way I was going to admit he was right.

Bayshore Drive was deserted out near the state forest, but as we neared the beaches, it started to get more crowded.

"North Beach would have a good view of what's going on," I told Frank over the headset.

"You're right," he agreed. "There seems to be a big crowd, too. Let's stop and take a look."

We turned our bikes down the ramp and found a place to park. A swarm of people crowded the beach, watching as the pirate ship headed for the Bayport docks. A lot of people in the crowd were holding up signs that said things like WELCOME BUCCANEERS! and PREPARED TO LOOT AND PILLAGE!

"Has everyone in town gone crazy?" Frank asked me.

I pulled my helmet off and shrugged. "Maybe." Then I spotted someone we knew in the crowd. "Chet!" I called, waving. "Chet Morton!"

Chet turned his big blond head toward us and waved back. "Yo!" he said. "Hey, guys!"

As Frank and I made our way through the crowd toward him, I noticed a pretty brunette standing at Chet's side. She smiled at me and I realized it was Iola, Chet's younger sister.

"Did you guys come to see the show?" Iola asked us. "Or are you going to try out?"

"Try out for what?" Frank said.

Chet rolled his eyes. "Where have you guys been, living in a cave somewhere?"

"Nah," I said. "We were in London chasing motorcycle thieves."

Frank shot me a nasty look. What I'd told them was pretty close to the truth—too close for Frank's liking. Of course the case we'd been on had started in New London, *Connecticut*, not London, England, but I knew Chet and Iola wouldn't believe me anyway.

"That explains your posh accent, Joe," Iola joked.

"But it doesn't explain what's going on," I said.

"It's *Buccaneers*," Chet said, "the biggest adventure challenge show on TV. You must have heard about it."

What can I say? ATAC keeps me and Frank so busy that we don't have a lot of time for television. "You mean the competitive reality show?" I asked.

"We've heard of it," Frank said. "Who hasn't?"

"But we've never watched it," I admitted. "Is this some kind of publicity stunt for the show?"

"Oh, man," Chet said, "I can't believe you guys don't know. This *is* the show! They're shooting in Bayport this week!"

"Every couple of episodes, they sail the ship into a new city and set up the game there," Iola explained. "They're auditioning local people for the show and shooting over the next few days."

"The show's been a hit all up and down the East Coast," Chet added. "But the game is so tough that no one has won the big prize yet."

"Really? Why not?" Frank asked. I could tell

my brainiac brother was interested, and I kinda was too—or I would have been, if I hadn't been so tired from the Kendallson case.

"To win the big prize you have to beat out all the other contestants," Iola said. "Then you have to finish a final obstacle course before the ship's cannons fire."

"A couple of people have finished the course, but not before time ran out," Chet explained.

"So they lost?" I said. "That stinks."

"Contestants win prizes along the way," Iola said.

"Some of the treasure they win is really cool," added Chet.

"Treasure?" I asked. Suddenly the show was sounding more interesting.

"Sure," Chet said. "If you get to the island phase of the game, you get to dig for real treasure. Some guy won a car last show."

"They buried a car?" I asked.

"Of course not!" Iola said. "They bury small treasure chests containing prize parchments."

"Sometimes they give away gold or jewelry, too," Chet told us. "One woman won enough to put her kid through college."

"People take the game very seriously," Iola added. "Some folks even go into training before trying out."

"But I'm betting some people just do it for their fifteen minutes of fame," I said.

Frank rubbed his chin. "So it's a lot like the game shows that are popular in Japan," he said.

Ugh! Leave it to my brother to come up with a comparison that you have to be in the nerd club to understand!

"Yeah. Pretty much," Chet said, confirming that he was a member of the club too. All the time we'd been talking, the pirate ship had been sailing closer and closer. Now it turned broadside to the beach and fired its guns.

Kaboom!

Frank and I both ducked, but no fireballs whizzed over our heads. The rest of the crowd cheered.

"I was right," Frank whispered to me. "It must have been a misfire when it shot at us before."

I nodded. In our profession you can never be too sure whether something is a coincidence or a serious threat.

"So," Iola said after the cheering had died down, "are you and Frank going to try out for the show?"

"A lot of people from school are going to give it a shot," added Chet. "Like Marty Sirkin and Daphne Soesbee."

"Daphne's trying out?" Frank said. "I thought she was more a brainy type than an athlete."

"The game requires brains as well as brawn," said Iola. "You have to be a good puzzle solver to pass some of the tests."

"What about you, Chet?" I asked. "Are you and Iola going to go for it?"

Chet shook his head. "I'm doing the armchair athlete thing this time."

"Trying out conflicts with my end-of-summer softball schedule," Iola said. "Otherwise I would. What about you, Joe?"

I shrugged. "The treasure part sounds interesting, but, to tell you the truth, Frank and I are kind of beat."

"We just got back from some heavy dirt riding," Frank explained.

"Well, they're having tryouts tomorrow morning, too. So you can still sign up then if you change your minds," Iola said, smiling.

I smiled back. "Yeah, maybe," I said.

"We'll think about it," said Frank. "Come on, Joe. Let's go home and hit the showers."

"Good idea," I agreed. "See you both later."

By the time we got home, I was more than ready to shower and crash for the night—even though it wasn't dinnertime yet.

Mom and Dad were just setting the table

as Frank and I walked in the back door.

"Have fun riding, boys?" Mom asked.

"Yeah, it was great," Frank said.

"Did you have any trouble with the trails?" Dad asked.

Our father is Fenton Hardy, famous investigator and, like I said before, one of the founders of ATAC. Someone else runs the group now, but Dad still keeps tabs on what's going on. His question was a kind of code, asking how the mission went.

"Nope," I told him. "We had a few bumps along the way, but nothing we couldn't handle."

Dad nodded. "Glad to hear it."

"Are you boys going to shower before supper?" asked Mom. She glanced at our dirt-covered riding clothes.

"That's the plan," I replied.

Just then Aunt Trudy appeared in the kitchen doorway. "Not so fast," she said. "Before you go upstairs, there's something you need to do." She looked really put out and concerned, which isn't unusual, because she frets over Frank and me constantly.

"What's up, Aunt Trudy?" Frank asked.

"There's a shaggy-looking pirate on the doorstep," she huffed, "and he says he needs to talk to you boys."

3. One Last Adventure

A pirate on the doorstep!

Joe and I exchanged a furtive glance.

"Is it Chet, up to one of his pranks?" Joe asked.

Aunt Trudy shook her head. "Morton I'd know," she replied. "Whoever this is, I didn't recognize him. He almost scared the daylights out of me!"

"Maybe he's here to see us about a parrot," I joked.

"Yeah, Playback is about due for his fifty-thousand-squawk checkup," Joe added. Playback is the parrot we adopted after one of our cases.

Aunt Trudy shook her head.

When we got to the front door, sure enough, a ragged-looking pirate was standing there.

"Who are you supposed to be, Johnny Depp?" Joe asked.

"Dude, do you really think so?" the pirate asked. Under his long hair, fake beard, and scraggly outfit, he wasn't much older than Joe and me.

"So, you came here to audition?" said Joe sarcastically.

"No," the pirate replied, "I came here because *you're* auditioning."

"What do you mean?" Joe and I asked at the same time.

"I mean you've won a free pass through the auditions of *Buccaneers*," the pirate said. "You get to be on the show!" He reached into his long, gaudy coat and pulled out a pair of tickets emblazoned with a golden *Buccaneers* logo. The tickets had our names on them.

"How did we win them?" I asked. "We've never even watched the show."

The pirate shrugged. "I guess you've got friends in high places," he said. "Oh, and there's a package that comes with it." He reached into his coat again and pulled out an envelope. Joe and I knew immediately that it had come from ATAC.

Joe took the package and nodded toward the stairs, indicating that we should go up to our room and check the assignment right away.

The pirate courier leaned close and whispered, "A plus on today's apprehension. C minus on the recovery of stolen goods, though."

"Hey, that motorcycle just got a little wet, that's all," Joe whispered back.

"At least the owners will get it back," I added. "That's more than they would have gotten if Kendallson had escaped."

The pirate shrugged again. "You know best, dudes," he said. "Catch you later." He waved half-heartedly as he turned and left. We closed the door and headed for the stairs.

"What did the pirate want?" Mom called from the kitchen.

"Something about that game show that's come to town," Joe called back.

"We'll tell you about it after our showers," I added. We sprinted up the stairs and into my room before Mom or Aunt Trudy could ask any further questions.

The minute the door was closed, Joe ripped open the package and a CD fell out. To anyone else, it would have looked like a normal video game. And, after we'd gotten our information from it, it would reformat itself to play like a regular CD too. But the first time we viewed it, we'd be getting the lowdown on our latest ATAC mission.

The label on the disc said BAYPORT BUCCANEERS.

I turned on the water in the bathroom to drown out any noise while Joe popped the disc into our game system. Immediately the screen filled with colorful images of pirates in swashbuckling action.

"Cool!" exclaimed Joe.

"These pirates aren't actors," I pointed out. One pirate had glasses, a lady buccaneer had a perm, and several of the cutthroats were wearing wristwatches.

"For regular people, they're doing some pretty outrageous stunts," Joe said.

The fake pirates swung from ropes, dived underwater for treasure, had swordfights, climbed to a crow's nest, and did all sorts of other stuff that stuntmen usually do in pirate movies.

As the scenes formed into a collage of wall-to-wall action, a skull and crossbones appeared on the screen. The skull zoomed forward, and, as it did, the title "Bayport Buccaneers" appeared.

An ATAC mission controller's voice said, *"As you might be aware, the TV show* Buccaneers *has come to Bayport to film part of its new season. The show casts ordinary people in the roles of pirates competing for treasure."*

"Yeah, yeah," Joe said, "we know. Get on with the assignment!"

My brother! He'd barely heard of the show an

hour ago, but to hear him talk, you'd think he'd been watching it all his life.

The mission controller continued. *"Competitors from all over the country are lining up to try to win the show's two-million-dollar top prize. Unfortunately that prize may have lured trouble to the show as well.*

"Recently, while filming in New Bedford, Massachusetts, the show's prop and set designer, Greg Olson, drowned while setting up a Jet Ski stunt. While the coroner ruled Olson's death an accident, the circumstances of the drowning remain suspicious. Since then more mysterious 'accidents' have plagued the show. Aside from Olson, no one has been hurt yet, and ATAC would like to keep it that way."

"I imagine the contestants would like to keep it that way too," I said.

"UAN, the network airing Buccaneers, *has asked ATAC to look into these incidents,"* the controller continued. *"The tickets sent with this disc allow you to bypass the show auditions and compete in the game. Your assignment is to mingle with the other contestants, find out whether the accidents are a case of sabotage, and—if they are—stop them. Good luck. This disc will reformat in five seconds."*

Joe turned off the player.

"Looks like we're going to be TV stars, bro," he said, grinning.

I scowled. "We'll have to work twice as hard to stay undercover with millions of people watching."

Joe scratched his head. "I hadn't thought of that," he said. "Leave it to my big brother to take all the fun out of stardom!"

I hooked my thumb at the bathroom. "You hit the shower while I do some research," I told him. "We need to maintain our cover with the family."

"Check," Joe agreed. "What are we gonna tell them about the show?"

"As much of the truth as we can get away with," I replied.

Fifteen minutes later we'd rinsed off and were ready for dinner. I'd uncovered some info about the show so we wouldn't look completely ignorant when we arrived on the set. Unfortunately I didn't turn up anything more about the accidents or Olson's death. I suppose the network had been doing its best to keep them quiet. But that meant Joe and I would be starting from scratch when we got to the set.

We sat down at the dinner table. "So, what's this about a game show?" Aunt Trudy asked after the food had been served.

"It's really cool," I said. "We won tickets to be on the show."

"That's great," Mom said. "What's it called?"

"*Buccaneers*," I said. "It's a reality show."

"They're shooting here in Bayport over the next couple of days," Joe added. "Starting tonight."

Mom frowned. "That's kind of last-minute notice, don't you think?"

"Yeah," Joe said. "Our tickets got lost somehow. That's why they sent that guy in the pirate costume down here, special delivery."

"So," said Mom thoughtfully, "is it just tonight that you'll be sitting in the audience?"

"Mom," Joe said, "we're not going to be sitting in the audience. We're going to be competing."

"Wait a minute," Aunt Trudy put in. "I saw something about that show on *Confidential Edition*. People have gotten hurt doing that show. They also said that there's a crime wave that follows the production around. Did you know that, until recently, the cities that have hosted the show reported a fifty percent jump in jewelry store robberies? Those people pretending to be pirates are taking themselves a bit too seriously, if you ask me."

Joe looked like he might blow his top. "Aunt Trudy," he said, "you can't believe everything you hear on those tabloid TV shows."

I kicked Joe under the table, trying to get him to calm down. Mom and Aunt Trudy were sure to gang up on us if we lost our cool. "Competing on the show shouldn't be any more dangerous than an average track meet," I said, fibbing. "And Joe and I compete in track events at school all the time."

Mom wrung her hands. "That's just what I'm worried about, boys."

"Track?" asked Joe.

"No," Mom replied, "school. School's starting soon. Rather than running around playing pirates, you really should be getting ready for the new year."

"But, Mom," Joe protested, "it's still summer!"

"And the shoot is only for a couple of days," I added.

"And we could win some prizes," Joe concluded.

"I agree with you, Laura," Aunt Trudy said. "It's too close to school for the boys to be starting an adventure like this. Besides, they could be hurt."

Nightmare! Mom and Aunt Trudy were ganging up on us.

Sure, they meant well, but if we couldn't compete in the show, there was no telling what kind of trouble might happen! Fortunately, at just that moment, Dad cleared his throat.

"I'm with the boys," he said. "It's still summer,

and they should have some fun while they can."

Good old Dad! He doesn't chime in much, so when he does, it really counts.

Mom slowly nodded. "All right," she agreed. "Go. Have some fun on your TV show. But be careful."

Yes!

"You bet we'll be careful," I assured her.

"We always are," added Joe.

"And keep your eye out for real pirates," Aunt Trudy warned. "I mean, people who are taking the game too seriously."

Just at that moment our parrot Playback flew into the room. "Real pirates!" he cawed. "Real pirates!" He settled down on his perch in the corner as the rest of us finished our meal.

Our excitement over the new mission made us forget our exhaustion completely, and Joe and I couldn't wait to get going. But wolfing down dinner wouldn't have made Mom or Aunt Trudy any less worried. So we sat, ate, and made polite conversation, just like any normal night in the Hardy household. As soon as the dishes were cleared and in the dishwasher, we revved up our bikes and headed downtown.

We pulled up in the big city park next to the dock where they'd tied up the fake pirate ship. The ship had looked cool sailing into the bay, but it was even more impressive up close. It was half as long as a football field and had three big masts with sails the size of circus tents. Rows of cannons stuck out of holes in its sides. The topmost mast, with its enormous pirate flag, looked to be a hundred feet tall.

"Welcome to Hollywood, Bayport style," Joe said as we parked our bikes.

"It'll be almost like starring in a movie," I replied, thinking of the clips we'd seen on the assignment disc.

Together we walked toward the crowd gathered in front of the dock near the ship. Hundreds of people were milling around, wanting to get onto the show. On the far side of the crowd one banner read AUDITIONS and another read QUALIFIERS. There were a lot more people in the auditions line.

Normally that's where Joe and I would have had to go, to try out for the show along with everyone else in Bayport. But thanks to ATAC, we got to skip that part. "Qualifier" was printed in big letters on the front of our tickets, right next to our names. We high-fived each other and headed for the second banner.

"Uh-oh," Joe said as we walked. "I see trouble."

Sure enough, lurking among the crowd of contestants was our archenemy, Brian Conrad.

4.
Eating Crow's Nest

Brian Conrad—just what we *didn't* need. But he always seems to turn up wherever Frank and I go. The only good thing about Brian is his sister, Belinda. She's a babe, and she has a serious crush on Frank. Unfortunately she wasn't with Brian at the docks.

There were a lot of people standing in line to try out, but Brian wasn't with them. He was standing in the line marked QUALIFIERS—the same line Frank and I were headed for.

Naturally, since we didn't want to talk to him, he spotted us right away.

"Well, if it isn't the Hardy dweebs," he said.

"Did they have a breakout at the zoo?" I asked Frank. "'Cause I sure smell something rank."

Frank sniffed the air. "Orangutan?" he asked. "Or maybe hyena?"

"Har-de-har-har," Brian said, which wasn't much better than the way he usually laughed. "Apparently they'll let anybody on this show."

"Just what we were thinking," I shot back.

Brian balled up his fist, and for a moment I thought he might hit me. I guess I didn't look scrawny enough for him to pick on, though, because the next minute he relaxed and said, "You guys aren't supposed to be in this line—it's for people who *already* qualified. Tryouts are over there." He jerked his thumb over to the other line.

"Then we're in the right place," I said, brandishing my ticket.

Brian went red in the face. "How'd you get that?" he said. "I didn't see you trying out!"

"We won ours in a contest," Frank explained.

"That figures," Brian said. "I spend half the summer chasing this show around, trying to get an audition, and you guys just waltz in without even trying. You Hardys sure have the luck! It's like you were born on a silver platter or something."

I ignored his bungled metaphor and shrugged. "Sometimes it's better to be lucky than good. Though, of course, it's better to be *both*." I smiled my most annoying smile at him. I figured if he hit me, they'd probably toss him out of the contest.

Brian didn't take the bait. "Well, then get to the back of the line where you belong," he said. "It's first come, first served here."

He turned away from us, and I can't say that I'm sorry he did. Any opportunity *not* to look at Brian's ugly face is an opportunity I'll take.

Frank and I found the back of the line and queued up. "Did you catch what Brian said?" Frank asked.

"About following the show around all summer?" I replied. "Yeah. I caught that."

"Maybe Brian's been causing a bit of trouble during his travels," Frank suggested.

"Could be," I said. Brian was a well-known troublemaker around Bayport. He was mean and quick-tempered, with a tendency to bully everyone he could. He'd caused his share of vandalism during the last school year—more than his share, actually. In fact Brian's middle name was Trouble, and everybody in school knew it. He practically lived in the vice principal's office.

"What would he gain by causing trouble for the show?" Frank wondered.

"Who knows?" I said. "Maybe he was mad 'cause they kept turning him down as a contestant. Breaking a few small things is just Brian's way of saying thanks."

SUSPECT PROFILE

Name: Brian Conrad

Hometown: Bayport

Physical description: Age 17, 6'2", 210 lbs., short blond hair. Dresses like a tough jock, because that's what he is.

Occupation: Full-time professional jerk.

Background: Grew up in Bayport in a not-so-nice family (except for his sister). Hobbies include pumping iron and working out. Spent his youth setting fires, causing petty vandalism, and picking on anyone smaller than he was. Still does all those things.

Suspicious behavior: Followed *Buccaneers* around all summer, trying to enter the competition. Causes trouble wherever he goes.

Suspected of: Sabotaging the show and causing a crime.

Possible motives: Wants the money. Wants the fame. Wants to show up his enemies-which is everyone.

"I don't know," Frank said. "I can see Brian sabotaging something to get back at the show, but drowning someone? That's too much, even for him."

"You're right," I admitted. "Assuming he did it on purpose. But wasn't Olson's drowning supposed to be an accident? Maybe Brian set up some prank and it went wrong."

Frank shook his head. "I'm still not buying it," he said. "It would require intelligence and planning."

I had to admit, that seemed to rule Brian out. "Okay," I said. "We'll just have to sniff around and see what we can find out about the death as well as the show's other trouble. Didn't the disc say the accidents started up after Olson died?"

Just then a woman with a clipboard and a megaphone appeared at the front of the line. She was attractive, in her late twenties or early thirties, and had shoulder-length brown hair done just so. She put the megaphone to her lips and said, "Good evening. My name is Marlene Krall, and I'm the producer and director of *Buccaneers*."

The crowd cheered, so we did too.

"If you're in this line, you've already passed an audition and gotten your ticket to appear in the show," Ms. Krall continued. "Anyone who does *not* have a ticket is in the wrong line. You need to join that crowd, over there." She pointed to the other, much longer line. "People in that line will still have a chance to compete in the show, but they'll be starting tomorrow morning. Those of you who already have tickets are starting tonight."

Another cheer, and this time I felt some of the crowd's excitement.

"In just a few minutes, you'll meet our host, Miles Stillman," Marlene said. "You may remember him from his roles in *Count Alucard's Death Cruise*, *Snakes on a Ship*, and of course *Bermuda Buccaneers*." Again, cheering. "But before you meet our star, we need to get you outfitted for the show. So if you all will stay in line and follow me to the costuming tent, our costumers and production assistants can get you started."

With that she waved her megaphone like a bandleader waving a baton and headed for a big tent staked up on one side of the park. The crowd followed after her, keeping fairly orderly—though I thought I saw Brian cut a place or two.

Inside, the tent was like a circus. There were long racks of pirate-style clothing, and people from the show—costuming assistants, I guess—were running around, checking tickets, and then handing out costumes.

No one came to help Frank and me when we got to the head of the line, so I stopped a pretty girl with bright blond hair as she dashed by.

"Hey, since everyone's so busy," I said, "maybe

we should just start on our own. If you can just tell us which costumes to pick from—"

"How should I know?" the girl said. "I'm not a costumer." I noticed now that she had a pair of heavy pliers in her hand, smears of paint on her jeans, a greasy blue rag sticking out of her pocket, and a heavy ring of keys at her belt. She definitely didn't look like a costumer.

"You'll just have to wait your turn," she said. "Excuse me." And with that she ran out just as quickly as she'd come in.

"That's a record for losing a girl, even for you," said Frank.

"I've seen *you* lose 'em faster," I shot back.

"Oh, yeah?" Frank retorted. He took a deep breath and stepped forward, aiming for a costuming girl with curly black hair. The girl was helping someone else, but Frank didn't seem to care. "E-excuse me," he said. "We need to get our costumes."

The girl smiled at him, if you can believe it. "I'll be right with you," she said.

Frank nodded, having used up his allotment of stammer-free words, and stepped back beside me. "See?" he said. "I did okay."

"Sure," I said, meaning just the opposite.

"At least my girl didn't run away," he pointed out.

We spotted some other people we knew in the

tent while we were waiting. There was Brian, of course, now decked out in—appropriately enough—a black pirate costume and hat, and Daphne Soesbee, too. She wore a maroon and white outfit that nicely complemented her red hair.

The costumer came over to us soon enough and helped us pick our sizes from the racks. The clothes, as it turned out, were pretty flimsy, kind of dingy, and held together with Velcro.

"With so many people to dress, they can't go for top-of-the-line costumes," Frank said. "I'm sure these will look fine on camera."

"They'd better," I said. "I wouldn't want to seem less than perfect for my public." I stuck my nose in the air and propped my hands on my hips, imitating a movie star pose.

"Who are you supposed to be, Johnny *Dupe*?" Frank asked.

"Better than being Depp Jam," I told him. "Look at you in that outfit! Dreadlocks don't suit you, bro."

Frank took off the wig the costumer had given him. "I guess I could lose this without them noticing," he said.

"You two," said a commanding voice from nearby. We looked over and saw the producer,

Marlene Krall, standing near the edge of the tent. "You look ready, and we need contestants. Head out to the ship."

Frank and I left the tent and went to the dock where they had the pirate ship tied up.

They'd made some changes while we were getting costumed. The ship now looked as much like a TV studio as it did a pirate vessel. A big neon *Buccaneers* logo blazed on the ship's landward side. The sails were gone, and a camera platform was attached to the main mast in the middle of the ship. Two sets of rigging, like big rope ladders, led up to the crow's nest. A metal gangway went from the crow's nest to the forward mast, and a set of spiral stairs led back down to the deck from there.

Maybe some of the other people in the crowd knew what to expect in this challenge, but Frank and I sure didn't. Before we could ask anyone, Marlene Krall climbed to the ship's bridge—in the rear, where the steering wheel was—and held up her megaphone.

"Okay, everybody, thanks for coming," she said. "We're about to start filming, so please remember that this is a TV show and be on your best behavior. Anyone who acts up will take a quick trip to the unemployment line, courtesy of our security chief, Jorge Alex Villatoro Junior." A burly security guard standing nearby nodded and smiled menacingly.

"Having said that," Ms. Krall continued, "we also want you to act like *Buccaneers*. Let's make this show fun, both for the viewers and for ourselves. And remember, you're only contestants on this show; the star is Miles Stillman." The crowd began to applaud, but she motioned for quiet. "Do what Miles says, remember your place, and I'm sure you'll have a great time. And of course you'll have a chance to win two million dollars."

Again, applause and cheers, along with a few piratelike growls of "Arrgh!"

"Okay," said Ms. Krall. "It's time to start the show. We'll count down from five and then roll cameras. Let's get it right on the first take!" She clambered off the ship and took up a position near a camera on the docks.

"Five . . . four . . . three . . . two . . . one . . . we're rolling!" Ms. Krall called.

Instantly a big man in a fancy pirate costume strode out onto the upper deck at the rear of the ship, near the captain's wheel. Everyone instantly recognized Miles Stillman and began applauding.

"Avast, ye swabs!" Stillman said in an over-the-top pirate voice. "Welcome to the Bayport edition of *Buccaneers*!"

Again the crowd broke into applause.

Stillman stared skeptically at the crowd on the docks. "I understand that some of you cutthroats think you have what it takes to join my crew. Well . . . we'll see. We'll see!"

The crowd kept clapping and shouting, "Arrgh!"

"I think what we need is a test to see who's worthy," Stillman went on. "More than one test, methinks. So first we'll start with a test of basic pirate seamanship. Every able-bodied buccaneer has to be able to climb to the crow's nest quick as lightning. So you're going to climb the rigging as fast as you can. That's a hundred and ten feet straight up, in case you were wondering. Are you ready?"

As one, the crowd said, "Aye, Captain!" Except for me and Frank, of course. We'd never seen the show and didn't know that was a catchphrase.

"Great! Cut!" Ms. Krall yelled. "Good job, Miles. We're moving on. You PAs, get the contestants in two lines and start them climbing. We'll go as soon as we're ready."

"Are you sure we shouldn't go again?" Miles Stillman asked. "I think I was a little hoarse on that one."

"You're a pirate, Miles," said Ms. Krall. "It was fine. Let's keep moving."

"PAs," as it turns out, is short for "production assistants"—a legion of faceless people who keep things moving behind the scenes of a show by doing whatever the producers tell them to. Two gals in *Buccaneers* T-shirts quickly got us contestants formed into two lines, next to the ladder-like rigging setups. More PAs, dressed as pirates, were stationed throughout the ship to keep things going. Two more, with stopwatches, stood atop the crow's nest, keeping time.

No sooner was the last person in line than the cameras were rolling again and Stillman started shouting, "Climb, me hardies! Climb!"

Contestants began climbing as fast as they could. The first two guys up had clearly come prepared. Despite their pirate costumes, they climbed quickly, hand over hand, from the deck to the top of the mast. The guy in the red beat out the guy in the blue by just a yard or so. Of course beating the guy you were climbing against wasn't as important as how fast you climbed.

Next came a blond girl and a guy I'd seen play football for Jewel Ridge, one of Bayport's rivals. The girl made it up okay, but the guy lost his footing halfway. He dangled by his hands for a few seconds before losing his grip.

I thought he was going *splat!* but he slid harmlessly

down to a big impact pad on the deck. I hadn't realized that every climber was safety-clipped to the outside line of the rigging.

The two climbers behind that guy had to dodge out of the way (which slowed them down a bit), but no one got hurt. Stillman, who was stalking around the bridge at the stern of the ship, laughed piratically as the guy fell and then shouted encouragement to the next climbers.

After climbing, the contestants walked across the gangway between the two masts and then down the stairs to the ship's bow.

From where Frank and I were standing, I couldn't tell what time we needed to beat to continue the game. We had to make it, though. ATAC was counting on us.

Frank and I were in separate lines, but we would be climbing the rigging at almost the same time—dead last. Unfortunately, through the luck of the draw, Brian Conrad was climbing right in front of me. I don't know which is worse, the sight of Brian's front or his back. I knew one thing, though: I was going to make it up to the crow's nest faster than he did.

Brian started, and when he got a third of the way up, the PAs gave me the go-ahead.

I started climbing, hand over hand, as fast as I

could. The rough, prickly ropes scraped against my bare palms as I pulled myself up.

No way was I going to let Brian beat me, though. He had a big head start, but as we went, I started gaining on him. I angled for the left side of the rigging, since Brian was on the right.

We were about twenty feet from the top. Brian was only a few rungs ahead of me now. He'd looked back and saw me getting close.

Then, without warning, the rigging lurched and something went *snap.* Fine, powdery dust sprayed around my head, and the ropes beneath my feet gave way. I glanced down as the huge swath of rigging below me fell to the deck.

I found myself dangling by one hand, clinging to a single strand of rope in midair. Brian saw the predicament I was in, but did he stop to help? You bet he *didn't*. He scrambled up to the crow's nest as quickly as he could, leaving me swinging.

I tried to get a grip with my other hand, but the rigging swayed like a loose hammock and I couldn't catch hold. The prickly rope was cutting into my palms; my fingers began to ache. Even worse, since the ropes had fallen away, my safety clip was now attached to *nothing*.

Without meaning to, I looked down. The people on the deck below looked like dolls. They were running around frantically, trying to figure out what to do.

But none of them could help me.

If I lost my grip, I was a goner.

5.
Rotgut Rigging

I was almost all the way up to the crow's nest when I heard a *pop* and then a loud *snap!*

I saw Joe dangling in the air, hanging on by one hand to the only rope left. He tried to swing up and grab hold with his other hand, but the rigging swayed precariously and he couldn't catch on. His knuckles went white; I knew he might lose his grip at any moment.

The PAs waiting at the top of the mast leaned down, extending their hands, but they were too far away to help.

I looked around frantically, trying to figure out some way to keep my brother from falling. A spar for hanging sails ran across the mast right near the top, just a foot above me. There were ropes attached to it for hoisting the sail. The ropes looked sturdy, and several hung all the way down to the deck.

I raced up that last foot, grabbed a rope, and unclipped myself from the rigging I was climbing. As Joe's grip loosened, I swung out between my rigging and his.

"Joe!" I called.

He turned and saw me just as his fingers gave way.

I swung into him, grabbing with my free arm. He grabbed me with both of his.

Oof! It felt like being hit with a sack of cement, but both of us held on. Joe's added weight caused the rope to swing back toward the rigging I'd been climbing.

We reached the netting, and Joe grabbed hold with one hand. He pulled us in until we could stick our legs through the climbing loops. I let go of the swinging rope and we both grabbed on tight. The rigging swayed precariously under our weight, but it held.

We scrambled up to the crow's nest as fast as we could.

"Thanks," Joe said, panting. "That was close."

I nodded; I was too out of breath to do anything else. The production crew rushed over and helped us to our feet. I checked the event timer; it looked bad. "Not quick enough!" I whispered to Joe.

"Don't worry about it," he whispered back. "At least we're alive."

"But how are we going to stay on this case if we can't compete?" I asked.

Disheartened, we walked over the catwalk to the far mast, and then down the spiral stairway to the foredeck. Everyone on the ship was cheering our narrow escape, but Joe and I barely noticed.

What we did notice was Marlene Krall racing across the deck of the ship. She didn't come to see Joe and me right away; she went to one of her cameramen first.

"Did you get that?" she asked frantically. "Did you get that?"

The cameraman nodded, but his face looked very pale. I think he was more scared than Joe and I had been!

Ms. Krall reached us just after we set foot on the foredeck. A bunch of PAs and other production people were crowding in, trying to make sure we were okay, but Ms. Krall pushed right through them.

"Are you boys all right?" she asked.

"We've been better," said Joe.

The answer threw her. "Do you need a doctor?" she asked.

"Nah," I answered. "We'll be okay."

"Good," she said, and then turned to the crowd. "All right, everybody, that's a wrap for the day! We'll pick it up again tomorrow morning—six a.m. for the others who are competing in the first round, ten a.m. for those who competed tonight. See you all bright and early!"

As the crowd began to disperse, she turned to one of her PAs and said, "Where's Clay?"

"Mr. Folwell?" asked the PA, a thin young woman with glasses. Her name tag read PAULA.

"Yes, of course," Ms. Krall snapped. "Clayton Folwell, our mechanic. We need to find out what went wrong with the rigging and fix it before filming starts tomorrow morning."

"Um, I think he may be resting," Paula said.

"Drunk is more like it," Ms. Krall grumbled. "If he's been drinking on the job again . . . And find me Sam Olson, too. If we can't make the rigging safe, we'll have to use another elimination challenge. I want to see what sets we have ready to go."

"Yes, ma'am," Paula said, darting off.

"What about us?" I asked.

"What about you?" Ms. Krall replied.

"We didn't make the time," I said. "Do we just go home?"

Ms. Krall looked shocked. "Go home? Of course

not! You boys gave us the best footage of that whole round. My sponsor would kill me if I sent you home. You've got a pass through to the next round, of course. But try to avoid any more heroics. *Buccaneers* is only supposed to *look* dangerous."

"Okay," said Joe, "we'll try not to be heroic the next time your set breaks."

"Good," Ms. Krall said, missing the sarcasm. "Since you're through the first round, we won't need you until about ten a.m. Please be on time for your next event."

"Right," I said. "C'mon, Joe." We climbed down to the main deck. Marlene Krall turned away and immediately began shouting orders at a nearby PA.

"So," I asked Joe as soon as we were out of earshot, "what do you think happened up there?"

"I think Brian cut the rigging somehow," Joe said hotly. "You saw how quick he got out of there once the ropes gave way."

"That's pretty extreme," I said doubtfully. "Way out of Brian's league."

"I wouldn't put anything past that guy," replied Joe. "Do you have another suspect?"

"What about that mechanic Ms. Krall was talking about—Clay Folwell?"

"What about him?"

"A drunken mechanic could cause an awful lot of problems on a TV show like this," I said. "We should talk to him if we can."

"We have to find him first," Joe said. As we made our way down the gangplank to the dock, we spotted the blond girl who had brushed Joe off earlier. She was hurrying past us toward the ship when Joe stopped her and said, "Hey, can you tell me where to find Clay Folwell, the mechanic?"

The girl laughed. "Clayton Folwell? Ha! If I knew that, Krall would give me a medal. Now if you'll excuse me, I need to talk to her."

"Are you one of Ms. Krall's PAs?" I asked.

The girl looked insulted. "I'm Samantha Olson, the show's designer," she replied. "I work on the sets and props."

"I thought Sam Olson was a man," Joe said, sticking his foot squarely in his mouth.

"Then I guess you need your eyesight checked," she replied.

"Samantha," I said, "are you related to Greg Olson, the man who drowned a while back?"

The girl's eyes narrowed and she glared at me. "I'm his *daughter*," she answered. "Excuse me." She pushed past us on the gangplank and headed toward the spot where we'd last seen Marlene Krall. Joe and I continued down to the dock.

"So Greg Olson had a daughter and she's working on the show," Joe said thoughtfully.

"Yeah," I said, "we definitely need to talk to her. She could be a gold mine of information."

"Let's let her cool down a bit first," Joe suggested. "I don't think we made a good first—or second—impression."

"You got that right," I said. "What do you want to do next?"

Joe rubbed his blond hair. "Why don't we look around the docks a bit—see what we can see."

"Yeah, okay," I agreed.

Rather than following the crowd out of the park, we headed toward the bay. The *Buccaneers* ship was tied up at the northernmost wharf in the marina. A line of other piers, some just as big, ran south from there, toward the Port Authority building. Access to the show's dock was restricted by security, but the other wharves were still open for public use. Joe and I walked past a boathouse and out onto the pier nearest the ship.

Because it was late, no other boaters or fishermen were on the dock. We walked past a couple of bait shacks and numerous boat slips out to the pier's end. From there we had a good view of the *Buccaneers* ship. Though the big floodlights had been shut off for the night, there were still plenty of people bustling around the ship's deck, preparing for the next day's filming.

"What's that out there?" I asked, pointing at a huge black shape out in the bay.

Joe peered into the darkness. "Looks like a barge," he said. "It's coming in awful late, though."

"It's not a barge," said a slurred voice from nearby. "It's an island."

Joe and I spun and saw a man sitting propped up against the back side of a bait shack. He'd been so quiet that we hadn't spotted him as we walked by. The guy was middle-aged, with about three days' growth of beard. He was wearing a plaid shirt and jeans. His breath reeked of alcohol.

"Who are you?" I asked, already suspecting the answer.

The man staggered to his feet. "Th' name's Folwell," he said. "Clayton Folwell."

"What do you mean, that's an island in the bay?" asked Joe.

"It's for the show," Folwell slurred. "It's Treasure Island."

"So it's a barge made up to look like an island," Joe said.

Folwell nodded. "Yup. Ironic, isn't it?"

I didn't see the irony. "Why didn't it come in with the pirate ship?" I asked.

"It's too slow," Folwell replied. "It's always hours behind the ship. That's why they never use it during the first day of filming." He hiccuped and winked. "I been out there, working on it, most of the day—before they called me to set up the rigging. It's full of treasure, you know."

"So how come you're not on the ship with everyone else?" Joe asked.

Folwell waved his hand at us dismissively. "They don't need me once filming starts. That's my cue to take some time for myself." He picked up a softball-size stone from where he'd been sitting and threw it out into the bay with all his might.

"But what if something goes wrong?" I said. "They had a problem on the set tonight."

"They did?" he replied.

"Yeah," Joe said. "Some of the rigging broke. A couple of contestants nearly got killed."

Folwell rolled his eyes. "Even with the crime wave over, the show's problems keep rolling on," he moaned. "And I'm sure Krall is blaming *me* for the trouble! Like I'm responsible for everything that happens on her set. Why can't she understand that other people don't want to work themselves to death the way she does?"

He steadied himself and began staggering back toward land. "I guess I better go see what went wrong with the set," he said. "But you know what? I really don't care. I don't need Krall or any of them. Not anymore. Because I've discovered the secret. I know who did it, and I've got the proof."

"What secret?" asked Joe. "What proof?" We were eager to find out what Folwell meant, so we helped support the mechanic as he staggered back toward the *Buccaneers* dock.

Folwell smiled drunkenly and said, "It's hidden. But it won't be much longer. I know where to find it."

"What's hidden?" I asked.

"Shhh!" Folwell whispered loudly. "It's a secret."

"But what is it?" Joe asked persistently.

"If I told you," Folwell replied, "it wouldn't be a secret."

We tried to get him to say more, but Folwell clammed up tight. When we got to the dock, Paula the PA thanked us for finding him, and then whisked the mechanic off to see Krall. We tried to tag along, but a security guard barred our way. "Sorry," he said. "Contestants aren't allowed back on the set until morning."

Joe looked like he might say something, but I pulled him away. Arguing with the show's guards would only make things tougher on us later.

SUSPECT PROFILE

Name: Clayton Folwell, aka Clay

Hometown: Burlington, Wisconsin

Physical description: Age 37, 5'9", 180 lbs. Dresses like an engineer, in flannel shirts and jeans. Looks like he's been drinking for a long time and has no intention of giving it up.

Occupation: Mechanical engineer on *Buccaneers*.

Background: Engineering degree from UW-Whitewater. Worked with the show since its beginning. Very good working with mechanical devices when sober. Divorced, no children.

Suspicious Behavior: Drinking on the job. Notably absent when needed. Doesn't seem bothered that his carelessness may cause danger to the show or to other people.

Suspected of: Shoddy workmanship that causes accidents.

Possible Motives: Neglect rather than intentional damage. Grudge against the show's producer/director or other people on the show.

"So what do you think Folwell was going on about?" Joe asked as we reached the parking lot.

"Maybe he found out who was causing the accidents," I suggested.

"Seems to me like *he's* the prime suspect," Joe said.

"Yeah," I agreed, "but then what does he mean he doesn't need Ms. Krall anymore?"

"Beats me. Maybe he's turning pro."

"A professional saboteur?"

"Sure," said Joe, not meaning it.

"Folwell said he found something," I said, "some kind of hidden proof. He said the crime wave was over, but not the trouble."

"What crime wave?" Joe asked. "Did he mean the accidents? 'Cause they're certainly not over."

"Do you think it has something to do with what Aunt Trudy mentioned earlier?" I asked.

Joe shrugged. "Beats me. I figured she was just overreacting to a tabloid news report. What now?"

"Now we head home," I said. "We're going to need as much rest as possible if we want to win this competition."

"Hey, winning would be great," said Joe, "but aren't we in this to solve the case?"

"Yeah," I said, "but we can't do that if we miss the cut and get kicked off the set."

"Then I guess we better win," Joe said, smiling.

We mounted our bikes and rode back home. After parking in the garage, we headed for the back door.

"Let's not mention the accident to our parents," I suggested as we walked.

"Yeah," Joe agreed. "No sense worrying Mom."

"Or Dad," I said. "Even though he's involved with ATAC, some of our assignments still make him nervous."

Joe reached for the doorknob, but as he did, the door swung open on its own.

Aunt Trudy stood on the doorstep in her bathrobe and pajamas. She did not look happy. "It's about time you got home," she said. "Didn't you think we'd be worried?"

"Worried about what?" I asked. I didn't get what she meant. It wasn't that late, and she knew we'd been at the docks working on the show.

She arched an eyebrow at Joe and me. "I know you two think all old people are senile," she said, "but we're not completely out of touch. Did you think we wouldn't hear about the accident on the news?"

Busted!

"I'm sure they made it sound worse than it actually was," I said.

"It *sounded* like you almost fell to your deaths!" Aunt Trudy told us. "They even had a video clip."

Double busted.

"Can we talk about it inside?" Joe asked.

"I suppose so," Aunt Trudy conceded, stepping out of the way.

Joe and I trudged past her and into the kitchen. "Sit," she commanded. We took seats at the table. Aunt Trudy sat down beside us and picked up her cup of coffee. Mom and Dad appeared from the other room and joined us.

Joe and I felt like we were in front of a firing squad. I wasn't sure that even Dad would be able to bail us out this time.

"The least you could have done was call," Aunt Trudy said.

"Honestly," said Joe, "we would have called if there had been anything to worry about. It was just a little accident, that's all. Things go wrong on TV shows all the time. If it had been really serious, we'd have let you know."

"Besides," I added, "we had to keep our cell phones off for the show. We can't have ring tones blaring out when we're supposed to be pirates." That was true, but I got the feeling that our parents and Aunt Trudy weren't really buying it.

"And what were we supposed to say if we called?" Joe asked. "'Hi, there was a little accident on the show, but we're okay and you shouldn't worry about it?'"

"Well, yes, as a matter of fact," Mom said.

"That would have been nice," Dad agreed.

Ouch.

Rather than getting ourselves out of trouble, we were sinking in deeper. One more wrong move and our *Buccaneers* mission would be over.

6.
A Ship Full of Suspects

No doubt about it, Frank and I were in it up to our necks.

"No matter what it looked like on TV," I said, "it was just an accident. And we're here, aren't we? So it wasn't that serious."

"Besides, it could have happened to anybody," Frank added. "And I'm sure they'll make certain that nothing like it happens again. The whole production crew was freaked out."

"Really?" Aunt Trudy said. "You couldn't tell it from that Krall woman's interview after the video clip. I almost thought she was pleased to get the attention."

"I think that's a little harsh, Trudy," Mom said.

"The show would be in big trouble if anyone got hurt."

"They'd at least have serious trouble with their insurance company," Dad put in.

"Sure they would," I said. "Which is why I'm *positive* no accidents like this will happen from now on."

"I certainly hope not," said our dad. He didn't look pleased at what had happened, but I could tell he wasn't ready to call off the mission—yet.

"Besides," I said, "I'd hate to quit now, just when we've advanced to the next round."

"Which won't do you a whole lot of good if you break your necks," Aunt Trudy grumbled.

"Despite what the news may have made it look like," Frank insisted, "the show's really well run. It's no more dangerous than riding a WaveRunner or a motorcycle."

"And we do those things all the time," I added.

"Statistically, it's safer," said Frank, trying to keep the momentum going, "since no contestants have actually been hurt while filming the show, and people are hurt all the time while riding."

Aunt Trudy crossed her arms over her chest and frowned. "And that's supposed to make us feel better, is it?" she asked.

"Actually," Mom said, "looking at it that way

does make me feel better. The boys are right. A lot of things teenagers do are more dangerous than being on a reality TV show."

"Right," I agreed. "More people have been killed by sharks than by *Buccaneers*."

"In the TV show sense of the word," added Frank.

Mom chuckled. "Well, since it *is* your last adventure of the summer, I guess we can let it continue."

"You have to keep us updated, though," Dad said, "if there's any more trouble on the set."

Aunt Trudy didn't look convinced, but she added, "We don't want to hear about it on the news first."

"You won't," I promised. "Now, if it's okay, we're going to hit the sack. We have to be on the set again tomorrow morning, so we need plenty of rest."

Dad nodded toward the upstairs. "Get going," he said, "before we change our minds."

Frank and I got up to our bedrooms as quick as we could. Both of us knew we'd dodged a bullet. We'd need to be doubly careful from now on—or we'd be off the case before it even began.

"I can't believe Ms. Krall released footage of the accident to the media," Frank said.

"I can," I said. "She's publicity hungry, and that

makes her the top suspect on my list."

"Mine too," Frank agreed. "Except maybe for Clayton Folwell. It wouldn't take much effort for a mechanic to set up an 'accident' like that. And we know he doesn't like her."

"Or maybe he's only *pretending* not to like her, and they're working together," I suggested.

Frank and I got up early and went to the docks before seven, even though we didn't need to be there until ten. We figured that showing up early would give us a chance to mingle with the *Buccaneers* crew and the other contestants.

Before the day's events started, Ms. Krall stood on the ship's bridge and introduced the show's main sponsor to the crowd. The man's name was Pedro Alvarado, and he was the head of Alvarado Gold, a company that made Mardi Gras coins, beads, and other party items.

"As many of you probably already know, Mr. Alvarado's company has funded *Buccaneers'* two-million-dollar top prize," Ms. Krall said. "So if any of you are lucky enough to complete the *Buccaneers* challenge, you'll be winning *his* money, not mine."

She grinned and clapped Alvarado on the back. He waved to the contestants, but his smiling face looked like a put-on to me.

SUSPECT PROFILE

Name: Marlene Krall, publicity hound

Hometown: Hollywood, California

Physical description: Age 33 (but trying to look 23), 5' 7", 120 lbs., brown hair, hazel eyes. Snappy dresser with perfect clothes and perfect hair all the time.

Occupation: Producer/director of *Buccaneers*.

Background: Born in Moline, Illinois, Marlene left home to do better than her parents had. She started with set construction and worked her way up through the television industry to become the producer of one of the most popular reality shows of all time.

Suspicious Behavior: Worrying about the show first and people's lives second, releasing sensational accident footage to the news media to get attention for the show.

Suspected of: Doing whatever it takes to keep *Buccaneers* at the top of the heap, including staging accidents to make a splash on the news.

Possible motives: Hungry for publicity, uncaring about people.

"You have to sell a lot of beads to make two million dollars," Frank said, echoing my thoughts.

"Yeah," I agreed. "I bet he's the only one who's happy that nobody has ever won the top prize."

"I wouldn't be too sure about that," replied Frank. "I bet the show's ratings will drop once someone *does* win. Until then the suspense just keeps building, and the audience with it."

Mr. Alvarado stepped off the ship's deck and mingled with the crew as Ms. Krall got the early-morning shoot under way.

They'd scrapped the rigging climb and added a new event—an obstacle course set up in the dock parking lot—for the remainder of the qualifying round.

"Somebody must have worked hard to set that course up overnight," said Frank.

"I'm betting I know who," I said, spotting a light blond head among the people near the ship.

Frank followed my eyes. "Samantha Olson," he said, nodding. "Yeah. Since she's the designer, it'd probably be up to her and the show's mechanic to get things done."

"Let's try to talk to her," I suggested. "She can't still be mad at us, and she might know something about what happened with the rigging last night."

Frank agreed, and the two of us pushed our way

through the crowd toward the ship. We skirted around the contestants waiting to compete in the obstacle course, but as we did, Frank tripped over an electrical cable.

Before he could stop himself, he stepped on the foot of a young woman dressed in a purple and gold pirate's outfit.

"Hey, watch it!" the girl squawked. Her dread-lock wig snapped around like a mane of whips as she wheeled on us. The name on her entry ticket read KENYA KRUGMAN.

"Sorry," said Frank. "I tripped."

"You shouldn't be here, anyway," Kenya said, "not unless you're competing." She hopped up and down on one foot, checking her other boot.

"We competed last night," I told her. "Are you okay?"

Kenya looked at us suspiciously, like she thought Frank might have stepped on her deliberately. "I think so," she said. "If I'm not, I'll be asking your lummox friend for my share of the prize money."

"I'm Joe Hardy," I said. "The lummox is my brother, Frank."

"Sorry," Frank repeated. "I didn't mean to."

"I don't care if you *meant* to," Kenya snapped. "I've been training for this show for a long time. The last thing I need is somebody lousing up my chance just when I'm ready to hit the big time."

"So you think you can win *Buccaneers*?" I asked.

"Count on it," she said confidently. "I'll do whatever it takes to win—including stomping back if guys like you stomp on me. Now get out of here. You're ruining my concentration."

"Sorry," Frank said again as we walked away.

Leaving Little Miss Attitude behind, we managed to get right next to the ship without any further mishaps. It wasn't hard to spot Samantha Olson among the crew. Her blond hair stood out like a beacon. Plus, aside from the PAs, she was about five years younger than anyone else working on the set. She was relaxing in a director's chair, sipping coffee, when we caught up to her.

"Hey," I said, "remember us? Joe and Frank Hardy."

She nodded, looking very worn out. "You're the guys who almost fell from the rigging last night."

"Sorry if I insulted you before, thinking Sam Olson was a guy," I said.

"Forget it," she said. "I was kind of tense last night, with the trouble on the set and the boss yelling for me and all. Plus I didn't know who you guys were then."

"You're pretty young for a designer, aren't you?" Frank asked.

"I've been doing props and sets for ages," she replied. "I worked with my dad before I finished high school."

"So you were already working on *Buccaneers* when he . . . ," Frank began. I almost thought he was going to put his foot in his mouth (my brother is good at that), but he stopped short instead.

"Yeah," she said. "I was working on the show with him when he died."

"That must have been tough," I said.

Samantha's blue eyes got very cold. "Dad was careless, and that's what got him killed. It wasn't the show's fault. I won't make the same kind of mistake."

"What do you think happened with the rigging last night?" asked Frank.

She shrugged. "Manufacturing defect on the ropes maybe?" she said. "I'm a designer. I don't handle that stuff."

"I thought you designed sets and props," I said.

"I design them, I don't *make* them," she explained. "That's Clay's job. Of course sometimes Marlene has me step in when he's . . ." She stopped in midsentence.

"You mean Clayton Folwell?" Frank said.

"When he's . . . what?" I asked.

"Sorry," she said. "I talk too much. Sometimes

Clay's . . . under the weather, that's all. Talk to him if you want to know more. You'll see what he's like."

"Do you know where he is?" asked Frank.

"On the ship or the island maybe," she suggested. "I don't know. His job takes him all over—when he's up for doing it. If I were you, I wouldn't waste time asking about the rigging—I'd have my *lawyer* do it." She smiled wryly. "Now, if you don't mind, I'd like to catch some rest until the next crisis."

"You think there'll be more trouble?" I asked.

She smiled at me. "When you're working for Marlene Krall, there's *always* more trouble," she said. "She makes her own when she can't find any. Sometimes I think the show would run a lot more smoothly without her."

"She's kind of a cold fish, isn't she?" Frank observed. "After the accident last night, she seemed more concerned about the show than she did about whether we were okay."

"She was that way when my dad died, too," said Samantha. "It's just her way. Eyes on the prize, all the time—that's our Marlene."

"Do you think she could have set up last night's accident to get publicity for the show?" I asked.

"Forget I said anything," Samantha replied.

"I'm just tired, that's all. Since Clay was under the weather, I was up all night helping put that obstacle course together."

SUSPECT PROFILE

Name: Samantha Olson

Hometown: Buzzards Bay, Massachusetts

Physical description: Age 19, 5' 4", 110 lbs., blond hair, blue eyes, in good physical shape from working with sets. Wears practical clothing: jeans and T-shirts along with a tool belt and keys for work.

Occupation: Designer of sets and props for *Buccaneers*.

Background: Apprenticed as a designer on *Buccaneers*, working with her father until he got killed. Took over his job after that.

Suspicious behavior: Seems to have a grudge against the show's producer, has ready access to the show's sets and stage equipment.

Suspected of: Sabotage.

Possible motives: Said her dad's death was accidental, but obviously has no love for Marlene Krall. Might secretly blame the show.

"Well, thanks," I said. "See you later."

"Yeah," she said. "Maybe. Good luck with the competition." She grabbed a *Buccaneers* baseball cap from nearby, pulled it over her eyes, and leaned back in her chair as if to take a nap.

Frank and I walked away.

"Let's poke around the ship, if we can," I suggested.

"Good idea," Frank agreed.

As we walked up the gangplank, both of us were amazed at how much the ship had changed from last night. All traces of the rigging challenge were gone. Instead there were bars and metal tubing stretching from the bow almost to the bridge in the stern. The tubes were bent in strange, snake-like shapes and suspended about ten feet above the deck of the ship. It looked like a maze, hanging in midair. A thick wire led from the edge of the maze down into a hatch amidships.

In the middle of the maze was Clayton Folwell, puffing and sweating and mumbling to himself as he worked on the metal. His eyes were bloodshot and his hands shook.

"Hey, Clay," the PA named Paula called to him. "Have you seen the treasure props for the diving challenge?"

Folwell looked up, seeming worried for a

moment. "I had to move 'em," he answered. "They were in my way. They're in the belly of the ship with the rest of the challenge stuff. I'll get 'em for you later."

"That challenge is next," Paula said. "We need them so we can set up."

"I told you . . . *later*," snarled Folwell. He scowled at Paula and went back to work.

"What do you think he's doing?" I asked Frank.

"That's the electric eel maze," Frank replied. "I researched *Buccaneers* online last night, before I went to bed. The contestants have to navigate from one end of the maze to the other while holding a metal pole. If they touch the metal 'eels' suspended above the maze, sparks fly and they're disqualified."

"Sounds dangerous," I said.

"It *looks* dangerous," said Frank, "but there's not a lot of electricity running through the metal eels—just enough to set off the flashes."

Just then Paula the PA spotted us. "Hey, you kids," she called. "Clear the deck! We're about to test the maze."

"Sure, no problem," I replied. Once we were out of her sight, I shoved Frank into the captain's cabin at the stern (that's the back of the ship). There was a hatch in the cabin with a ladder leading down into the ship's belly.

"Why'd we come in here?" he asked.

"Folwell said the challenge equipment was in the belly of the ship," I reminded him.

"So?"

"Maybe we could get a look at the ropes that broke last night," I said.

"Good idea," Frank agreed. "Let's go."

The area below deck looked like a messy hardware store. Wires and sheet metal and pipes and pieces of sets were scattered everywhere. Obviously the production company used the belly of the ship as a warehouse for all the sets and supplies needed on the show.

We saw treasure chests of all sizes, fake swords, plastic palm trees, a net full of fake coconuts (which we could tell were fake because most were broken in half), a bevy of stuffed parrots, axes, ladders, ropes, skeletons, hammocks . . . just about everything you could imagine a pirate might want or need.

"I can see why that PA couldn't find those treasure props down here," I commented.

"Check out the fancy power plant," Frank said, pointing. "I guess they need it in case the port they tie up in doesn't have enough juice for their gear."

I looked to the stern and saw an area blocked off with yellow wire mesh. A big red and white sign on the mesh said DANGER: HIGH VOLTAGE. Behind the mesh, a huge generator hummed away. Beside it stood an electrical panel with a series of outputs, each labeled with a different voltage. Obviously the generator had to run a lot of different appliances on the show.

"That green cable was running to the eel maze, wasn't it?" asked Frank.

"I guess," I said. Leave it to Frank to pay attention to a stray wire! "Why?"

My brother pointed inside the electrical cage. "Because the green cable isn't running to one of the low power outlets," he said. "It's running to the *high voltage*. There's enough power in that line to electrocute someone!"

"Maybe they have a transformer to reduce the voltage before it electrifies the eel maze," I suggested.

"I didn't see a transformer on deck," Frank said, "and I don't see one down here, either."

"Well, let's just pull the plug then," I said, reaching for the thick green cable.

"Stop!" Frank cried. "That could be *live*, for all we know."

I stopped. "We'll cut it off at the source then." I tried to open the reinforced mesh door to the generator cage, but it was padlocked shut. "No good!"

"We have to warn them," Frank said urgently.

"Hurry!" I said. "Before someone gets killed!"

7.
Shocking Developments

Joe dashed toward the stern of the ship, with me right behind.

We raced up the ladder and into the deserted captain's cabin. We pulled on the door . . . but it didn't open!

"Someone's locked it!" Joe said. We couldn't break it down because the hinges were on our side.

"Make some noise," I suggested. "Try to get the crew's attention." Joe and I began shouting and pounding on the door.

Outside, contestants were still running the obstacle course. Cheers and applause filtered in to us through the cabin's portholes.

"I don't know if they can hear us," said Joe.

"They have to!" I said. "People's lives are at stake!"

We kept pounding and shouting. "Let us out! It's a matter of life or death!"

What seemed like an eternity later, someone finally opened the door. A very puzzled-looking Paula stood in the doorway. "What are you kids doing in here?" she asked.

"Stop the test of the eel maze!" I cried.

"Stop the test?" she said. "Why?"

"We think there's too much voltage running through it," explained Joe. "Someone could be electrocuted."

"But Mr. Folwell is testing it out himself," Paula replied.

We looked over her shoulder and saw Clayton Folwell wobbling his way through the maze. He held a steel pole tightly in one hand, trying to keep it from touching the eel-like metal tubes running overhead. Folwell moved the pole through the fake eels, concentrating hard. He didn't see us at all.

A bunch of PAs were standing on the deck, watching and applauding as he went.

"He's doing it on a dare," Paula explained. "He bet someone he could make it all the way through."

"Mr. Folwell, stop!" I cried.

"Drop the pole and get out of there!" called Joe.

Just at that moment the crowd in the park watching the obstacle course challenge roared.

"Those metal eels could be deadly!" I shouted, but I knew Folwell couldn't hear me above the cheers.

Folwell swerved and swayed. He looked drunk, and he clearly wasn't worried about touching the pole to the electrified eels. He had no idea he was taking his life in his hands.

I looked for the green cable, hoping I could find some way to unplug it from the maze. I spotted the cable near the far side of the deck. I'd have to run through the maze and past Folwell to reach it.

Could I do it without endangering him? I wasn't sure. Joe looked around desperately, but he clearly didn't have any better ideas. I steeled myself to try it.

Outside the ship the crowd roared again—louder this time.

Folwell must have heard them, because he turned toward the sound. As he did, the metal pole swayed sideways and touched one of the electrified eels.

ZAP!

Folwell gasped and sparks flew from the maze.

Everyone on deck stopped what they were doing, and for a moment the whole ship fell silent.

"Pull the plug!" I yelled.

A PA on the far side of the ship dived forward and threw a breaker switch near the maze entrance. The sparks stopped flying, and Folwell collapsed to the deck.

"Call 911!" I shouted. Everyone on deck reached for his or her cell phone.

Joe and I raced to Folwell's side, hoping all the power to the maze had been cut. We tried our best to revive the mechanic, but it was no use.

By the time the ambulance arrived, Clayton Folwell was dead.

Marlene Krall and Pedro Alvarado dashed onto the deck alongside the paramedics.

"What's going on here?" Mr. Alvarado demanded.

"Who's hurt?" Ms. Krall asked.

"It's Clay Folwell," I said. "He's been electrocuted."

"Something went wrong with the wiring for the eel maze," Joe added. "He didn't stand a chance."

Other members of the crew, including Samantha Olson and Miles Stillman, were gathering around the deck now as well.

"But Folwell wired that maze himself," Ms.

Krall said. "He wouldn't have made that kind of mistake, unless . . ."

"Unless what?" Alvarado asked.

"Unless he'd been drinking," Samantha said, completing Ms. Krall's thought.

"He definitely smells of alcohol," one of the paramedics confirmed.

"Will he make it?" Ms. Krall asked.

The paramedic shook his head and pulled a sheet up over Folwell's body.

Ms. Krall turned away.

"I—I won't have my company blamed for this," Mr. Alvarado said. "We've put a lot of money into this show—too much to have this kind of thing happen. I've half a mind to pull my sponsorship and shut the whole thing down!"

Ms. Krall rounded on him, anger blazing in her eyes. "You can't do that!" she said. "This season is critical to us. We need to complete these episodes to get reruns in syndication! Besides, you can't quit on us. We have a contract."

"The contract's no good if you can't film the show," Mr. Alvarado said.

Ms. Krall stared daggers at the sponsor. "We didn't stop the show during that unfortunate string of robberies," she said, "we didn't stop when Greg died, and we're *not* going to stop now."

"You're wrong about that," said a deep, firm voice. Up the gangplank came Officer Con Reilly, Officer Gus Sullivan, and a handful of Bayport's finest. "This show is shut down until we've determined what happened here," Con went on. The police officers with him immediately began taping off the crime scene.

"But we have a schedule to keep," Ms. Krall exclaimed. "We have obligations to our sponsors and the network!"

"Those obligations will have to wait until we're finished," Con Reilly said.

"A shutdown could mean bad press!" Alvarado protested. "I've got plenty sunk into *Buccaneers*, and I can't afford any more!"

"A man's been killed here," Reilly said. "And until we find out what happened, I don't give a hoot about money or networks or anything. If you want to complain, take it up with my captain. Until then I'll need each and every one of you to make a statement."

The police rounded up all the people on deck and everyone who had witnessed the accident or might have known anything about it. They spent the rest of the morning interviewing people—including Joe and me. We told our story pretty much as it happened, though we pretended we

SUSPECT PROFILE

Name: Pedro Alvarado

Hometown: Scottsdale, Arizona

Physical description: Age 43, 5' 8", 210 lbs., dark hair and eyes, wears hair slicked down. Wears nice pinstripe suits and expensive shoes.

Occupation: Degree in mechanical engineering from MIT. Owner of Alvarado Gold, manufacturer of fine trinkets. Grand prize sponsor on *Buccaneers*.

Background: Alvarado worked his way through school before getting a job in a plastics plant. He decided that he could do better manufacturing plastic trinkets for Mardi Gras and other celebrations and started his own business.

Suspicious behavior: Seems to care more about money than about people.

Suspected of: Sabotage or complicity in sabotage. Murder, or maybe manslaughter.

Possible motives: Has too much money sunk into the show already. Maybe doesn't want to give away that two-million-dollar prize. Can't get out of his sponsorship contract unless the show is shut down.

were just snoopy contestants looking around the ship rather than ATAC agents on a mission. ATAC is so secret, even our friends in the police department don't know about it.

During a break in the questioning, Joe and I called home, making sure we talked to Dad rather than Mom or Aunt Trudy. We knew that Dad would cast the accident in the best possible light when talking to Mom. He was concerned, but he understood that we were on a mission. After talking to him, we mingled with the other *Buccaneers* contestants and the show staff.

Most people seemed conflicted about what had happened. They were concerned about Folwell's death, but nearly everyone wanted the show to continue. Only a few contestants, including Kenya Krugman, seemed to know about the show's past troubles.

"In a competition like this, there are bound to be accidents," Kenya said. "So a few people get hurt now and again. That's life. The rest of us have to tough it out and keep going."

I didn't much like that philosophy, and I could tell Joe didn't either. We kept our lips buttoned, though, and our ears peeled for more info.

After our encounter with Kenya, we found Paula the PA. Unfortunately she couldn't remember who had dared Folwell to walk the electrified maze.

"There were a lot of people around," she said. "Everyone was busy."

"Tough it out" seemed to be the show's rallying cry. Whether it was because they were loyal or because they needed the work, most of the staff seemed to want the show to go on. Only Samantha Olson was more cautious. As we stood outside the production tent, we heard her talking with the show's major players. We found a secluded area nearby, where we could see and hear everything, and did some eavesdropping.

"We should start again only after we've checked all the sets and mechanical equipment," Olson told Marlene Krall. "I hate to say anything bad about him, but it was Clay's carelessness that caused this accident. We need to check everything he's done before we resume shooting."

"That could take weeks," Pedro Alvarado argued. "Maybe it would be best to shut down entirely. If anything else happened, think of the bad publicity we'd all get."

"Shut down when we're getting all this attention?" Krall replied. "I don't think so. You're not getting out of your contract that easily, Pedro. Yes, we'll check all the mechanical effects over, but as soon as the police will let us, we'll start shooting again. I'm hoping for tomorrow." She turned to Paula and added, "Have the studio call the Bayport police and try to hurry along the investigation. We want this done as soon as possible."

"Yes, ma'am," Paula said. She pulled out a cell phone and went to find a quiet place to make the call. Joe and I ducked out of the way as she walked past. She didn't see us, and we kept listening.

"Are you sure this is best?" asked Alvarado. "Maybe we should quit while we're ahead. None of us have lost money yet, and—"

"And we won't so long as we keep our heads," Krall said. "Not to seem cold about it, but this incident will bring us more publicity than we could buy."

"But I'm not sure I want my company associated with this kind of thing," Alvarado said. "I've got a lot riding on this."

"All of us do," Krall said. "Which is why we have to stick together. I know that two-million-dollar prize is a stretch for your company, but it's nothing compared to what we can make if we just hang tough. We can ride this wave or let it sink us. If we ride it, we'll be doing better than we ever have—Alvarado Gold included."

She turned to another PA, a young guy with curly black hair. "Round up the contestants. Tell them we'll start again as soon as we can. Have them hang by their phones and wait for the call." The PA nodded and began talking to the contestants nearby.

"Start checking out the props, sets, and rigs we need for the next segments," Ms. Krall told Samantha. "We don't have time to hire a replacement for Clay, so you'll have to fill in. I want everything ready to run by the time the police conclude their investigation."

"What about you?" Samantha Olson asked. "What are *you* going to do?"

"I'll talk to the media and try to put the best face on it," Krall said. "I'll be tearful but determined. You know, the usual song and dance."

Joe tensed up beside me. "The usual song and dance!" he whispered. "It's like she doesn't care that Folwell got killed! I bet she was this way when Samantha's dad died, too."

"Take it easy, Joe," I whispered back.

"Hey, guys," the curly-haired PA called to us.

We'd gotten so wrapped up in listening that we didn't spot him approaching. Thankfully he didn't seem to notice that we'd been eavesdropping.

"Shooting's over for now," he said. "The boss wants you to go home and hang by the phone. We'll call you once we start again."

"Okay," I said. "We'll wait for your call. C'mon, bro." I grabbed my brother's arm and pulled him toward the parking lot.

"Shouldn't we keep snooping around?" he whispered. "See if we can find out anything else?"

"We'd only arouse suspicion if we're still here after they've cleared the scene," I replied. "Like it or not, we'll just have to wait this one out."

"I'll wait," said Joe, "but I definitely won't like it."

We stopped at the costume tent, turned in our pirate outfits, and then headed for our bikes.

As we did, Marlene Krall walked toward a row of TV cameras, dabbing crocodile tears from her eyes. It seemed that for people like her, the show would always go on—no matter what the cost.

JOE

8.
Diving for Dollars

Paula the PA called the house early the next morning. The police investigation was over and the show was on again. It's amazing how a little pressure from Hollywood can speed things along.

The last contestants were just finishing up the obstacle course when Frank and I got there. Kenya Krugman was stomping around, looking proud and clutching her ticket for the next round. Miles Stillman prowled around the course, shouting encouragement to the pirates-in-training who hadn't finished yet. Frank and I went to the costume tent and got dressed.

When we got out, Marlene Krall was pacing back and forth on the deck of the ship, looking nervous.

Pedro Alvarado stood nearby, looking just as edgy as his producer.

"C'mon," I said to Frank. "Let's get close to the ship and see what we can hear." Trying not to attract any attention, we made our way through the crowd up to the ship.

We reached the gangplank at the same time as Samantha Olson. She looked tired and dirty.

"Hey, Samantha," I said. "What you've been up to?"

She smiled weakly at me. "Working with the PAs all night to get this next event set up," she said.

Marlene Krall spotted Samantha and came down the gangplank to talk to her. "Is it ready?" Marlene asked.

"I'm feeling tired, but otherwise okay," Samantha replied. "How are you?"

"I'm sorry," said Marlene. "I've been so worried about keeping things running that it seems like everything else slips my mind. Are you all right? Would you like some coffee?"

"No thanks," Samantha said. "It would just keep me awake, and I intend to crash once the next game is under way. Maybe sooner." She shot the producer a wry smile.

"So you found the missing treasure props?" Ms. Krall said.

"Yeah," Samantha replied. "I don't know why Clay moved them, but Paula turned them up. She said they're all in place."

"So is the game working? Is it *safe*?" Ms. Krall asked.

"Yeah, it's fine," Samantha told her. "It's great. The camera will love it. I personally vouch for its safety."

"Are you sure?" Ms. Krall asked.

"Who do you think I am, Clay?" Samantha asked. "Of *course* I'm sure. I checked the whole rig over personally. It's in the water and ready to go. It'll look great on camera, and you'll name your first kid after me. Satisfied?"

"Samantha, you're a lifesaver!" Marlene declared.

"Remember that when you see the overtime on my next paycheck," Samantha said.

"Don't worry," Ms. Krall said, "I'll remember. We'll even give you a special thanks in the credits for this episode—right before the dedication to Clay."

"I'm honored," Samantha said. But she seemed more tired than honored.

"Well, let's get this going before anything more can go wrong," Marlene said. She turned to the nearest PA. "Gather the contestants. I want to start the treasure diving event within the half hour.

Make sure that Miles is ready to go too."

"He likes an hour break in between segments," the PA reminded her.

"Well, we'd all like more time than we have," Ms. Krall replied, "but the scheduling troubles make that impossible. Bring him a sandwich, a pillow to sit on, whatever it takes. Just see that he's ready."

She turned and looked at Frank and me. "What are you two waiting around for?" she asked.

"We just wanted to know when the next event was starting," said Frank.

"As soon as possible," Marlene answered. "You should stay with the other contestants. It's safer, you know—and it will make my insurance company happy. Now shoo! We're very busy."

Frank and I went back to where the rest of the contestants were assembling. "You know," he said, "even though she tried to sound like she was kidding, I think Ms. Krall meant it when she told us to scram."

"Yeah," I agreed. "And what she said about us being 'safer' with the other contestants . . . is she really worrying about the insurance issues, or did she want us out of the way for another reason? Does she know more about the accidents than she's letting on?"

Frank shook his head. "I don't know. We'll just have to keep our eyes and ears open."

Naturally the first person we ran into after leaving the ship was Brian Conrad. "Are you still here?" he asked when he saw us.

"Funny," I said, "we were going to ask you the same thing."

"There's only been one event," Brian said. "I ain't been disqualified yet. But you guys didn't even finish the climb. Why are they letting you hang around?"

I couldn't take the look on his smug face. "The reason we didn't finish was because *someone* cut the ropes after you climbed up!" I said. "Maybe *you*!"

"In your dreams," Brian replied. "If you think I had something to do with it, prove it!"

"Don't worry," I said. "We will." Frank put his hand on my shoulder and tried to guide me away, but I wasn't going.

"You two are deluded," Brian jeered. "It's only a matter of time before everyone in Bayport figures it out."

"And it's only a matter of time before everyone figures out what a lying creep you are!" I shot back. I would have jumped him right there, but Frank held me back.

"Sure, brainiac," Brian said to Frank, "keep

your kid brother from getting beat up. What wimps you guys are! Why my sister likes you, I will never figure out."

Frank's face reddened, and for a moment I thought he might let me go.

"Hey, hotshots," said a cocky voice. "Save it for the competition."

All three of us looked up as Kenya Krugman walked toward us. "You boys are gonna need every ounce of testosterone you've got in the upcoming events." She smiled and laughed tauntingly.

Now it was Brian who turned red. "Mind your own business, girlie," he snapped. "This is between them and me."

"Sure," Kenya said. "I'll mind my own business. Go ahead. Beat each other's brains out. It'll save me the trouble of defeating you myself." She laughed again and walked off.

"Fighting with Brian could get us disqualified," Frank whispered to me. "We have to stay cool."

He was right, and I knew it. Unfortunately Brian figured it out as well.

"You guys are *so* lucky," he said. "Guess I'll have to beat you in the game." He stalked off into the crowd.

"Good thing Kenya stuck her nose in," said Frank.

"She's trying to psych us out too," I told him. "She's just a lot smarter about it than Brian."

"She'd have to be, wouldn't she?" Frank asked.

Both of us laughed.

Marlene Krall appeared atop a big platform set up beyond the obstacle course. "Is everybody ready for the next challenge?" she called out.

"Yes!" the crowd roared back.

"All right," Ms. Krall said. "Next up is Diving for Treasure—one of the most popular challenges on the show. We've used it every season, and this season is no exception."

Again, big applause. Frank and I joined in. We'd had time to research the show more overnight, and we now knew about the challenges the show had done before.

"We've set up the diving course in Barmet Bay, just off the stern of the ship," explained Ms. Krall. "Contestants will assemble at the far end of the dock. On a signal from the captain, you'll jump into the water and search for treasure. While all of you will go into the bay, there's only treasure enough for *half* of the contestants. If you come up with a piece of treasure, you're in. If you don't, then you're out. The PAs will be talking to each of you—explaining the rules, checking release forms and qualification tickets, and so on—before you jump in. Got it?"

"Aye!" the crowd bellowed, in true pirate tradition.

"Okay, then," Ms. Krall said. "Please make your way to the end of the dock. Take your time. Everyone who qualified will get to dive."

It took about half an hour for everyone to reach the end of the dock and have their papers checked. All of us pirates removed our boots so we'd be able to swim better. Ms. Krall called, "Action!" and the cameras started rolling.

Captain Stillman stalked around the end of the dock, overacting—as usual.

"So you've passed the first test, eh?" he growled.

"Aye, Captain!" we all responded.

"Ye still think you've got what it takes to be a buccaneer?" he said.

Again, "Aye, Captain!"

"Very well, then. To join me crew, ye must dive for treasure. Those who come up with treasure get to try the next challenge; those who don't . . . well, let's just say that Davy Jones's locker may have some new guests tonight!"

Stillman's crew, a bunch of PAs, and technical people dressed up as pirates all laughed evilly.

"One last warning," Stillman said, fixing his eyes on us. "The treasure is guarded by dangerous sea creatures. Beware, lest ye become lunch!"

Some of our fellow contestants murmured uneasily.

"I bet that's what Samantha Olson was working on," Frank whispered to me, "sea monsters."

I nodded. The show had done diving events before, but this was a new twist. "The monsters might be more dangerous than they've planned," I whispered back. "Be careful."

"Are ye ready, ye scurvy dogs?" Stillman asked.

"Aye, Captain!" we all replied.

"Then on the count o' three. One . . . two . . . THREE!"

With that, all the contestants leaped off the pier into the water. Some people dived like pros, others jumped awkwardly, a few belly flopped. Frank and I went in headfirst. The cool water sent a shock through my body as I hit.

Bayport had done a great job cleaning up Barmet Bay in recent years. The old factories had closed down, and nearly all the pollution was gone. The water was still murky, though, and the salt stung my eyes.

The channel was fifteen to twenty feet deep here with a sandy bottom, perfect for treasure hunting. I looked around, trying to sort the competitors from the underwater cameramen and find some treasure.

I spotted something glittering on the bottom, next to a giant clam shell. I kicked down toward it. As I got near, though, the clamshell opened and a blast of bubbles squirted into my face.

Startled, I lost my breath. As I headed for the surface, someone in purple and gold swam past me, heading for the treasure I'd seen.

I came up, gasping for air, and took a deep breath. Before I could go back down, Kenya Krugman surfaced beside me, a glittering piece of emerald jewelry clutched in her hand.

"Thanks for setting off the trap for me, sucker!" she said, and swam for shore.

I was steaming mad as I dived back under. Why hadn't I figured out the trap? There were no giant clams in Barmet Bay! This was obviously one of Olson's gags. I needed to be smarter if I wanted to keep going in the game. Only half the contestants would move on, and—thanks to Kenya—I'd just lost a chance.

Lots of people were surfacing with treasure as I went down again, but a lot more were resurfacing without. The rules said that you couldn't fight another contestant for a piece of treasure, but that didn't mean you couldn't scoop up something someone else dropped. I saw Brian snatch something a girl lost hold of before I surfaced the second time.

Frank came up next to me, clutching a pearl necklace. "Good work, Frank!" I said, trying not to feel jealous.

"Got anything?" he asked.

"No. I got skunked by the giant clam."

"Try closer to the pier," he suggested. "I thought I saw something shiny over there."

I nodded and went back under, heading for the pier. Sure enough, there was a piece glittering on the bottom, right near one of the big posts.

There was something else, too, though—a dark, tangled shape lurking among the pylons. At first I thought it was just a mass of seaweed. As I swam closer, though, I saw that it was a giant octopus!

Other contestants had spotted that treasure now too. I could see them swimming for the pier. I didn't have time to surface for another breath. I swam straight for the treasure.

As I did, the octopus's tentacles flashed toward me. They hit me in the face and shoulders. They weren't hard, more like big balloons. They didn't hurt, but they might have startled the breath out of me if I hadn't faced the giant clam earlier.

I ignored the tentacles and pushed through. The octopus blew bubbles in my face as I grabbed a gem-encrusted golden necklace from the bottom. By then, though, I hardly had any breath.

I headed up, clutching the jewelry in my hand. My lungs were nearly bursting by the time I broke the surface. I thrust my hand up into the air, holding the necklace tight.

From nearby, I heard my brother shout, "Yes!"

He swam up to me, and both of us headed for shore.

"That was one of the last pieces," Frank said. "I'm glad you got it."

"Me too," I said. The necklace's gold and rubies glittered in the morning sunlight. I knew it was just a prop, but it really looked like real treasure. And after what I'd gone through to get it, it felt like real treasure too.

The production people had hung a rope ladder from one of the piers so the contestants could climb out of the water.

Frank and I scrambled up it, only to find ourselves face-to-face with Captain Miles Stillman.

The fake pirate glared at us.

"You've violated the Buccaneer Code!" Stillman said. "It's the end for both of ye!"

9.
Thrown to the Sharks

"What?" Joe squawked. "We didn't do anything!"

"If it's because I told him where to look for the necklace . . . ," I began.

"Be quiet, Frank!" said Joe. "We got the treasure, see? That's what counts." He rattled the fancy golden necklace in his hand at the pirate captain. "Nobody said anything about contestants not helping each other!"

"Aye, you've got treasure, but whose treasure is it?" Stillman demanded.

"Whose treasure . . . ?" I asked. "What do you mean?"

The pirate pointed an accusing finger at us. "You stole that treasure!" he said.

"We did not!" Joe snapped.

"All treasure in this bay rightfully belongs to *me*!" Stillman said. He turned to a band of buccaneers at his side. "Seize them, me hardies!" he said.

The pirates all around us surged forward, grabbing at Joe and me. Both of us started swinging, but there were a whole lot more of them than us.

Before we could even get in a couple of good blows, they had our arms behind our backs. We kept struggling, though. Then I recognized one of our assailants; it was Paula, Ms. Krall's production assistant. Suddenly what was happening began to make sense.

"Joe!" I whispered. "This is all part of the act!"

"I know that," he whispered back. "Did you think I didn't know that?"

Yeah. Right. He didn't know it any more than I did. This was another new twist to the show.

We kept struggling, but not quite as hard; we wanted to put on a good act, after all.

"Get your hands off me, you sea dogs!" Joe said.

"I'm innocent! I protest!" I added. "I've always been true to the Buccaneer Code!"

Eventually the pirate crew subdued us and tied our hands behind our backs. Then they dragged us back to the dock next to the ship.

Joe and I were the last qualifiers out of the water,

so most of the other contestants were already on the deck when we got there. Every one of them—including Brian and Kenya—had been tied up. Some were still putting on a show of struggling against their pirate captors; others awaited their fates quietly.

One by one, the pirate crew led us up the gangplank onto the *Buccaneers* ship. The Treasure Island barge was anchored right next to the ship. A tall platform had been built on the fake island. It was connected to the ship by a gangplank. Costumed pirates stood atop the platform, jeering at us captives.

A huge circular tank full of water sat on the island, beneath the long plank. Dark shapes circled in the water and triangular fins cut the surface.

Sharks!

The tank was filled with hungry-looking sharks!

"Now, ye scurvy knaves," Captain Stillman said, "prepare to walk the plank!"

"They're not really going to make us walk over those sharks, are they?" Joe whispered to me.

"It looks like they are," I replied.

"But that's crazy!" he said.

What could I say? I agreed with my younger brother, but both of us knew that we had to participate in whatever insane stunts the show threw at us. It was the only way to stay on *Buccaneers*, and the only way to keep our mission going.

I stared at the board over the shark-filled tank. It would be tricky to walk with our hands tied, but I felt certain that Joe and I could handle it. "Just keep your cool," I whispered to him. "We can do this."

"According to the laws of the sea," Captain Stillman explained to the contestants, "the last of the accused pulled from the water will be the first to walk." He pointed to Joe and me. "That means this pair goes first. Take the rest of the prisoners below to wait their turn."

The production assistant pirates rounded up the other contestants and led them down through a hatch in the center of the ship until only my brother and I remained.

"Are you ready, ye scurvy dogs?" Captain Stillman asked.

"Bring it on," Joe said.

Stillman smiled, showing several gold teeth. "Then take one last good look," he said.

"One last look at what?" I asked.

Before I could find out, several crew members stepped forward and wrapped a blindfold around my head. Other pirates did the same to Joe. The crew chuckled menacingly as they made sure we couldn't see.

"Hey!" said Joe. "How are we supposed to walk a plank that we can't even see?"

"You think it's too hard, do ye?" said Stillman's piratical voice. "Perhaps you'd rather abandon ship altogether. Is that what ye want?"

"No," I said. "We'll do it."

"Even if it's not fair," Joe added.

I couldn't tell if my brother was nervous about the test, but I sure was. I know that most sharks aren't dangerous to people—in most situations. But when a person suddenly falls into the middle of a school . . . ? I didn't want to find out.

"Not fair, ye think?" Stillman said to Joe.

"No," I assured him. "It's fine." I didn't like the tone in Stillman's voice. He was cooking something up. "Let's get going," I said.

"I've decided you're right," said Stillman suddenly. "It's not fair. For buccaneers of your caliber, this test is far too easy! Help them onto the plank, me hardies!"

With that, Joe and I were grabbed by several sets of pirate hands. The buccaneers pushed and pulled us around the deck, up and down stairs, and all around the ship until I didn't have any idea where we were. Then, just to make certain, they spun us around few times before setting our feet on the plank.

"There!" Stillman said. "That's better. I'm sure this is a much more suitable test for pirates like you. Get to the other side, and ye move on to the next challenge. If not . . . !"

He and the other pirates laughed.

"You first," Stillman said roughly, pushing me forward.

My bare toes hit the edge of the plank. I stumbled, and the pirates laughed, but I regained my footing.

The board had seemed pretty wide the last time I'd looked at it, but now—with my hands tied and my eyes blindfolded—it seemed as narrow as a balance beam.

"Go slow," Joe whispered from behind me. "They're not timing us."

"Right," I whispered back. "Just stick with me and we'll be fine." I tried to sound confident for my younger brother, but that's not how I felt.

In my mind I could see that big tank of sharks, circling below us. Each of them must have been eight feet long. I didn't know what kind of sharks they were, but any shark that size can take a good chunk out of you if it wants to.

I inched my feet forward and tried not to think about it.

I knew the far side was only about thirty feet away, but it seemed like miles.

I heard the water below me, slapping up against the side of the ship. The sea breeze tugged at my hair and pressed my baggy shirt against my skin.

SUSPECT PROFILE

Name: Miles Stillman

Hometown: Chicago, Illinois

Physical description: Age 43, 6' 2", 180 lbs., shaved head, in good shape—obviously works out

Occupation: Actor, currently playing the *Buccaneers* captain.

Background: Began work as a stagehand. Got his break when a stunt actor fell sick. Had a string of hit movies a couple of years back, but hasn't been getting the prime parts lately. Definitely working on *Buccaneers* for the money, but Hollywood rumors say that it's hurting his career.

Suspicious behavior: Enjoying his role as cruel pirate captain too much.

Suspected of: Cruelty to contestants, possible sabotage, possible murder.

Possible motives: Bitter over being stuck in a contract that's no longer good for his career.

I felt with my toes for the edge of the board, first one foot, and then the other.

"Easy, now," I muttered to myself. "Take it easy."

"Argh! What's taking ye so long?" Captain Stillman bellowed. "Face your death like a buccaneer! The way you're dawdling, you'd think ye were afraid!"

I tried not to listen to him, tried to keep concentrating on the plank. But searching for the edge of the board, I stuck my right foot out too far to one side. My bare toes found only air.

I tried to pull back, but my heel caught on the edge of the plank.

I pitched forward, trying to regain my balance, but it was too late.

Before I knew it, I was tumbling through the air.

"Frank!" Joe yelled from above me. Though he'd been just a couple of feet behind me, he seemed miles away.

Air rushed past my face and then I hit. The salty water splashed up around me, and I plunged headfirst into the shark tank.

10.
The Brave and the Dead

My heart froze and I stood stock-still as I heard Frank hit the water.

What was I supposed to do? My big brother had just fallen into the shark tank. He was out of the game—and maybe out of the mission—but more importantly, he was in danger.

I knew a show like this couldn't really let people be eaten by sharks. They must have fed the sharks recently, so Frank should have been relatively safe.

On the other hand, the eel maze *should* have been safe too—but it killed Clayton Folwell.

Going after Frank meant abandoning the mission. But if I finished the contest and let my big brother get eaten by sharks, what would I tell Mom and Dad?

Taking a deep breath, I jumped off the side of the board.

The water slapped my feet hard as I hit. Instantly I plunged in over my head.

I pulled at the kerchiefs tied around my wrists. Fortunately the buccaneer crew hadn't tied them very tightly—it was only a game, after all—and I'd been working on loosening the knots anyway, just in case.

It took only a few moments for me to twist my hands free. As I kicked for the surface, I tugged at my blindfold. At any moment I expected to feel a shark's teeth chomping on my leg.

Something brushed against my calf. I kicked hard, and my foot hit something. The shark didn't bite me, so I must have scared it off. How long would that last, though?

I came up, gulped air, and then dived back down, ripping the blindfold off as I went. I looked around. The tank seemed much larger now that I was inside it. I couldn't see the circular walls at all.

Happily I didn't see any sharks, either. I saw Frank, though, struggling underwater nearby. He'd gotten his hands free too, and as I kicked toward him, he pulled off his blindfold as well.

He looked around and spotted me. I pointed

to the surface. Both of us did one last check for sharks and then swam up as fast as we could.

As we broke the surface and gasped for air, the pirate crew whooped and laughed.

We had come up about twenty feet from the rear of the *Buccaneers* ship—almost in the same spot where we'd been diving for treasure. We weren't in the shark tank at all!

"They *tricked* us," Frank said.

I was thinking the same thing. "Once they got us dizzy, they took us to a *different* plank."

"It was still a pretty dangerous stunt," Frank said.

"We could have drowned," I agreed.

"Did you kick me?" Frank asked, rubbing his side.

"Sorry, bro, I thought you were a shark."

We swam back to the rope ladder we'd used earlier and climbed out. Once again Captain Stillman was there to greet us.

"Did ye have a nice swim?" the actor asked.

"Great," I said, rolling my eyes.

"Arrgh, no hard feelings, then," Stillman said, offering me a hand up. I resisted the urge to pull him into the bay.

"So what was the point of tricking us into thinking we were walking over the shark tank?" asked Frank.

"This was a test of bravery," Stillman explained, "and you two have passed. You're on to the next challenge, and as a special reward, you get to keep the jewelry you recovered during your dive."

He handed back the necklaces we'd recovered.

"Thanks," I said, not really meaning it. A fake gold and ruby necklace didn't seem like much of a payday for jumping into what I thought was a tank full of sharks. Frank didn't seem too happy with his faux pearls, either.

"Aye, you're welcome," Stillman said. "Get yourselves dried off and be ready for the next test." He turned and stalked back toward the ship. "Bring up the next victims!" he cried. The cameras went with him.

"Dry off in the costume tent," Paula told us. "You can watch the rest of the contest from there."

"Why can't we watch from the ship?" I asked.

Paula smiled. "Because we want the others to think you've been eaten by sharks," she said.

We went into the costume tent, where they sat us down in front of some heaters and near a TV monitor.

As we dried off, we watched the other contestants walk the plank. A whole bunch of people chickened out. They got up to the deck, saw no survivors on the far side of the plank, and just ran away. Others opted out after the crew blindfolded them, but not Brian or Kenya Krugman.

Brian, of course, was as dim as a five-watt bulb. He'd walk into a wall of rotating knives if you told him there was money on the other side. I was starting to wonder about Kenya's IQ, as well.

She actually ran, blindfolded, all the way to the end of the board before discovering she had nowhere to go and falling into the drink. The guy following after her tried to turn around and go back, but the pirates pushed him in when he reached the ship. His bad luck to go swimming and still not pass the test.

Brian didn't even make it halfway. The girl in front of him reached the end of the plank and found there was nowhere left to go. She shrieked and fell in. That scared Brian enough that he tried to turn around. He missed his footing, though, and wound up in the bay. He kicked and sputtered in the surf, shouting for help until the crew pulled him out.

Of course that's not the way he told it once he reached the costume tent.

"I knew it was just a test," he bragged.

"Sure you did," Frank said sarcastically.

"You guys are such dopes!" Brian said. "Did you really think they'd feed us to the sharks?"

"I saw the look on your face as you fell, Brian," I said. "Your pants were wet even *before* you hit the water."

He lunged at me, but Samantha Olson, who was walking by, stepped between us. "Back off!" she said, laying her hands on both our chests and pushing. "If the boss sees you two brawling, you'll be kicked out even if you *have* passed the tests!"

"She's right," Frank said.

Samantha smiled. "Besides," she said, "you need those costumes dry *and* in one piece so you can be in the final scene for the day. Now, be good." She gave Brian such a sweet look that he shut up and backed away.

Paula came over, in case Samantha needed help. She put her hand on my shoulder and I sat down. Samantha moved Brian to a seat on the far side of the TV viewing area.

"Lucky she came by to keep you out of trouble," Frank whispered.

"Thanks, Mom," I replied.

The plank-walking event finished up just about the time the sun was setting. The show had started out with nearly two hundred people; now fewer than fifty remained.

The crew gathered the survivors in front of the ship for a last shot. We were supposed to hold up the costume jewelry we'd won for the camera to see, but I couldn't find mine.

"Maybe it fell out of your pocket," Frank suggested.

"I thought I had it on," I replied.

"Well then, maybe you lost it when you and Brian were tussling," he said. "We can go back to the tent and look for it afterward."

"Or maybe Brian took it!" I muttered. I shot a look across the crowd of contestants to Brian, but I didn't see the jewelry on him. How low can you get, stealing someone else's prize!

"Are ye ready to move to the next competition?" Captain Stillman asked in his booming pirate voice.

"Aye, Captain!" we all replied, as Marlene Krall had instructed.

"Good!" Stillman declared. "Tomorrow we'll see what you swabs are really made of!"

"I hope he doesn't mean that *literally*," Frank whispered to me.

The set shut down for the night. Frank and I checked the costume tent but couldn't find the necklace I had won. The thought that Brian had taken it really burned me up, even if it was only a worthless trinket.

Frank and I wanted to hang around, but Ms.

Krall's PAs were on the prowl, and we didn't get the chance. So we went home. It was nice not having to worry about fibbing to our parents about what we'd done that day. Sure, we'd *thought* we were going to be eaten by sharks, but that danger had been entirely in our own minds.

Unfortunately we hadn't made much progress on the case. Who was sabotaging the show? Was the same person responsible for the deaths of Clayton Folwell and Greg Olson? Did he or she have something to do with the secret Folwell claimed to have discovered? Why was the saboteur (or saboteurs) causing so much trouble? Frank and I checked the Internet for more information and turned up something I never expected.

"Joe, take a look at this," my brother said.

I went over to his computer and my jaw dropped. There, on his monitor, was a picture of a fancy gold and ruby necklace. It was the same one I'd recovered from the bay—the same one I was sure Brian had stolen from me.

11. Dueling Buccaneers

Joe looked like I could have knocked him over with a feather. I'd been sorting through dozens of photos of priceless jewelry when I came upon his prize.

"According to this," I said, "that necklace was one of the pieces stolen in the robberies that Aunt Trudy mentioned."

"You mean that 'crime wave' supposed to be following the show around was real?" Joe asked.

"That's what it looks like," I said. "There was a whole string of jewel robberies when the show first started shooting, but it ended a couple of months ago."

"So they caught the criminal?"

"Not according to this," I replied. "They didn't

recover the loot, either." I rubbed my chin and thought hard. "Why would someone put a stolen necklace in the *Buccaneers* diving contest?"

"Beats me," Joe said. "But what if the robberies are the *real* cause of the trouble on the show? What if the stolen jewels are what got Clayton Folwell killed—and maybe Greg Olson, too?"

"You think that's the secret Clay found?" I asked. "That'd make sense, since he was talking about the proof freeing him from Ms. Krall and the show."

"Finding a fortune in stolen jewels could give someone financial independence," Joe agreed.

"So could blackmail," I said, "if you knew who stole the jewels in the first place. Which means whoever committed those robberies might be part of the *Buccaneers* crew."

"Or one of the people who's been following the show around," Joe suggested. "Someone like Brian Conrad."

"Do you really think Brian is smart enough to pull off a series of jewel robberies?" I asked.

"He stole the necklace from me, didn't he?" Joe replied. "Why would he risk taking it if he didn't know it was real?"

"Just to tick you off," I suggested. "Maybe he figures it will give him an edge over us in the competition."

"Maybe," Joe said. "But he's going to have to try a lot harder than that if he wants us off the show."

The ship had been overhauled again when we arrived early the next morning. The platforms and planks were gone, replaced with ropes and more rigging. A blue pirate flag flew from the bow of the ship, while a red pirate flag flew from the stern. Cameras were perched in the crow's nest to get a bird's-eye view of the day's event.

Paula and the other PAs checked papers and gathered all the contestants on the dock next to the ship. Joe and I decided to keep as far away from Brian as possible—at least until we figured out how to nail him on the stolen necklace. That put us next to Kenya Krugman, but I'll take a tough competitor over an enemy any day.

Pretty soon Marlene Krall appeared on the bridge of the ship. "Welcome back, everyone," she announced. "This is going to be another exciting day of competition here on *Buccaneers*. I hope you're all ready for action, as you'll be going sword-to-sword in a battle royal today. You won some small tokens yesterday, but today's winners will get a chance to really go for the gold.

"Unfortunately, as always, the losers will be sent home," she continued. "Look to your right and left. Chances are, if the person standing next to you doesn't go home for good tonight, you'll be going home for good yourself. Remember that when you're competing. Play hard, and play fair. Got it?"

"Yeah!" the crowd shouted in unison.

Kenya Krugman turned to Joe and me and smiled. "Boys," she said, "prepare to get your butts kicked."

In true pirate fashion, the teams for the upcoming game were determined by drawing straws. Luckily Joe and I ended up on the same side—the red team. Kenya ended up with us too, but Brian drew the blue team.

"Perfect," Joe said when we found out Brian would be on the opposite side. To Kenya he added, "I guess you won't be kicking our butts after all."

"Not in this contest," she replied. "But next time, watch out!"

The rules of the game were pretty simple. The red team and the blue team represented pirate factions, each in control of one side of the ship. Each team would have to cross the ship and capture the other team's flag, while at the same time defending its own flag from the opposing team.

The blue team would start in the bow of the

SUSPECT PROFILE

Name: Kenya Krugman

Hometown: Bayport

Physical description: Age 18, 5' 8", 125 lbs., dark hair and eyes, buff and toned—clearly a health-freak gym rat. Pretty, but way too intense. Wearing purple and gold pirate's outfit with long dreadlocks.

Occupation: Student.

Background: Kenya's about to start her last year of high school. She's hoping for an athletic scholarship but needs a backup plan in case she doesn't get it.

Suspicious behavior: Pushy and arrogant. Has said she'll do anything to win.

Suspected of: Mowing down anyone who gets in her way.

Possible motives: Wants the money. Hates losing.

ship; the red team—ours—would start in the stern. Each team got color-coordinated bandannas to put around their heads so you wouldn't fight the wrong contestants. Whichever team got the enemy flag back to its own end first was the winner. Stillman explained what would happen after that during one of his on-camera bits.

"The team that wins will continue their buccaneer tests; the team that loses will be going home. Some, I venture, will be going home in *caskets*." He laughed a piratical laugh, and the fake crew laughed along with him.

Clearly, if Joe and I wanted to keep working on the case, we needed to be on the winning team.

Naturally there were rules about how we could capture the flag. There could be pushing and shoving but no punching or kicking or stuff like that. Each contestant was given a prop cutlass made out of realistic-looking plastic. The swords were rigged with red paint inside them. When someone got hit, the sword left a paint mark that looked like a cut. The cutlasses weren't as hard as steel, but you still didn't want to get whacked with one if you could avoid it.

Judges dressed as pirates would be stationed throughout the ship. By looking at the amount of paint on a contestant, they'd determine who was "too badly wounded to continue." The wounded players would be out of the event, but they might still continue in *Buccaneers* if their team won the competition.

"The rewards for this competition are greater than ever," Stillman told both the camera and the contestants. "The jewels you won yesterday were mere trinkets—hardly real treasure at all. But those of you who survive today's battle will get a chance to dig for *real* loot on Treasure Island!" He pointed enthusiastically to the fake island anchored near the ship. "The prizes buried there include a brand-new Ford Escape Hybrid!"

The crowd of prospective buccaneers, including Joe and me, whooped and cheered.

"If we watch each other's backs, we should be okay," I told Joe as our team assembled on the ship.

"Remember," Stillman said, "you're supposed to be buccaneers, so act like 'em! The most daring team, whether red or blue, will surely win the day!"

Joe and I and all the rest of the contestants knew what that meant: The show was looking for cool swashbuckling during the battle. The crew had hung a lot of ropes to swing on for just that purpose and padded the booms and spars to make them less dangerous.

"Let's give 'em a good show!" Joe whispered.

"You bet," I agreed.

"Are ye ready, me hardies?" Stillman bellowed.

"Aye, Captain!" we all cried.

"Then let the battle royal begin!" Stillman cried. He lowered his black pirate flag and all the contestants jumped into action.

The teams had gotten a little time to plot strategy

before the filming began, and our team—the reds—had decided to leave the bigger and slower players in the stern to guard our flag.

The faster contestants, like Joe, me, and Kenya, would head forward and go after the blue flag. If any of us got "killed," another member of the team would take our place. Our team started out equally divided between attackers and defenders.

When Stillman lowered the starting flag, we ran down onto the main deck from the bridge. The blue team seemed to have adopted a similar strategy to ours. A bunch of them were also staying back to defend, while a group about the same size headed to the attack.

Brian Conrad was one of the attackers. Naturally Joe angled straight for him.

The two of them met near the middle of the ship and swung their swords at each other. They clashed, parried, and then took a step back.

"I want my necklace back!" Joe said to Brian.

"What are you talking about, Hardy?" Brian shot back.

"The necklace you stole yesterday," Joe said, swinging for Brian's head. "Did you know it was valuable when you stole it? Were you in on that rash of jewel robberies?"

This wasn't the strategy Joe and I had talked

about, but there was no way for me to stop him now.

Brian parried Joe's sword and tried to cut him on the backswing. "You're crazy!" Brian said. Joe ducked away, and Brian's sword slashed a trace of red down his sleeve.

"Watch out!" I said, parrying another blue team sword aimed at Joe's back. As usual my younger brother had gotten so focused on what he was doing that he'd lost track of everything else—including the blue team girl coming up behind him.

Joe turned, and the two of us fought with two other members of the blue team for a minute. Brian took that moment to escape. He headed for the bridge and our team's flag.

Joe and I landed a few good hits on our new opponents, but not enough to put them out of the game. They didn't get any paint on us before falling back to try another route. Joe and I looked ahead, to the red flag. There were a lot of people between us and it, but with some hard work, I knew we could get there.

"Hey!" Joe said suddenly. "Brian's put a razor or something in his sword blade! Check out what he did to my shirt!"

I looked. Sure enough, there was a clean slice in Joe's shirtsleeve, as if he'd been hit with an actual sword. The red paint on the sleeve made it impossible to tell if Joe had actually been hurt.

"Are you cut?" I asked.

"No," he replied, "but I'll cut Brian down to size once I catch him."

I knew that if Brian and Joe got into it, they might both get disqualified. And while I would have been happy to see Brian kicked out of the game, I needed Joe's help if we were going to crack this case. "Forget about Brian, Joe," I said. "I'll handle him. You go get that flag."

My younger brother stared at me for a moment, as though he wouldn't do it. Then he said, "Yeah, okay." He turned and jumped across the hatch in the middle of the ship. He landed on two members of the blue team, knocking them over.

I looked for Brian and found him climbing the steps to the ship's bridge. Two red defenders were trying to stop him, but I had to admit, Conrad was pretty good. He parried one sword and then cut across the chest of the guy on the stairs in front of him.

A long streak of red appeared on the guy's shirt. "Hey!" he said, looking down at the slash of paint.

"Out!" said one of the judges. "You're too wounded to continue."

The guy looked puzzled but moved out of the

way, dabbing his fingers at the paint. I hoped he hadn't been cut the same way Joe had, but there was no way to tell from where I was standing.

I grabbed a nearby rope, reeled back, and swung, hoping to intercept Brian before he got to our flag. My aim was good. I landed on top of the steps just as Brian shoved a contestant over the side. She hit the water with a resounding splash.

"Can he do that?" one of the players on our team asked the judge.

"I don't see why not," I heard the judge reply as I lunged at Brian.

Brian sneered at me and parried. "I've been aching to fight you for a long time, Hardy," he said.

"You'll be aching when I'm done with you," I replied. I slashed at him, but he parried. He slashed at me, but I brought my sword up in time. He ripped his sword away, and a tiny chip fell off my plastic blade.

Joe was right! Brian had put a razor in his sword!

Brian cut at me again, but I ducked under it. I put my shoulder into his chest and shoved him back. The air rushed out of his lungs with a satisfying *whoosh*.

I jumped back and swung my cutlass at him. I caught his arm and traced a red streak down his sleeve, but it wasn't enough to put him out of the game.

He caught me on the follow-through and put a similar slash on my sleeve near the shoulder—except in my case, the cut was real; it went through the fabric of my costume and nicked my skin.

I leaped back as he cut at me again. They'd hung a lot of swinging ropes around the set. I grabbed one, swung in an arc, and landed behind him.

Brian twirled and parried as I cut at him. "Ha!" he cried. "Not so tough without your brother around, are you?"

I ignored the taunt. With that razor blade in his sword, Brian was too dangerous to play with. There were only a couple of people, besides me, between him and the red flag.

He sliced right at my face, though they'd told us not to aim above the shoulders. The judges didn't see the cut, though, and I parried it anyway. "Anything to win, eh, Brian?" I said.

Our swords locked up momentarily, and he snarled at me, "You bet!" He shoved me back and I landed hard against the aft boom—the crosspiece connected to a tiny sail in the rear of the ship. The boom had been lashed to one side so it wouldn't hinder the fighting. That gave me an idea.

Brian could have lunged for the red flag near

the ship's wheel, but he kept going after me instead.

I jumped forward and caught his sword on mine as he came at me. We shoved at each other as I maneuvered into the position I wanted. Then I stepped back suddenly.

Brian lurched forward but caught himself before I could attack. He slashed at me, but I expected that. I ducked, and his sword hit a rope behind where I'd been standing. The razor in Brian's sword cut through the rope. I hit the deck.

As I did, the sail boom swung over my head, right at the startled Brian Conrad. Before he could react, the boom caught him in the midsection and swept him overboard. He squawked like a parrot as he fell into the bay with a resounding splash.

I smiled and leaped to my feet just as Joe and Kenya Krugman, together, swung onto the bridge deck, carrying the blue flag between them. A huge cheer went up from our team. We'd won!

All the members of our team—including the ones who'd been eliminated from the fight—gathered on the bridge, jumping up and down and celebrating.

Captain Stillman, who had been watching the contest from the shore, stalked onto the ship and up onto the bridge next to us. At about the same time, Brian Conrad slogged up the gangplank, sputtering and dripping water. He was still clutching his razor-rigged sword, and he looked as mad as a nest of wet bees.

"Congratulations," Stillman said both to us and to the cameras. "The red team advances to the next test. As for the blue team . . ." He cackled. "Well, I think the blue team would have preferred to walk the plank . . . again. They're *out* of the competition."

Most of the blue team hung their heads and grumbled, but Brian spoke up. "That's not fair!" he called out. "I eliminated half of those guys!"

"Hey, that's him!" said the red team guy Brian had slashed earlier. The show's medics were tending a suspicious cut on the guy's chest. "He's the one who cut me during the fight!"

"There's something funny about his sword," Joe said. "He cut my shirt, too."

"And don't forget about that boom rope," I added. "Everyone saw how he cut through that."

Apparently, in the heat of the moment, it hadn't occurred to the producers that Brian had cut through the rope. They'd been too busy filming exciting shots of him falling overboard. Now, though, Marlene Krall stared daggers at Brian.

Before Brian could get away, the show's security guards closed in around him. This was one tight spot our archenemy wasn't about to wriggle out of.

JOE

12.
A Slippery Challenge

How much better can life get? Kenya Krugman and I capture the enemy flag and win the game for our team. We get to move on to the next challenge, a challenge with real prizes. (Not that the piece of jewelry Brian stole from me *wasn't* a real prize.) And then, just to top things off, Brian gets dunked in the drink and caught red-handed.

Yes!

Today was turning out to be a very good day, and we hadn't even had lunch yet.

The show's security guys examined Brian's sword and found the razor hidden inside. I don't know what Brian was thinking when he put that blade in there. Maybe he just wanted to cause more trouble for Frank and me. Whatever he intended, it backfired.

"I don't know anything about that!" Brian screamed as the cops took him away.

Yeah. Right.

"I've been framed!" he cried. "Those Hardy boys have framed me!"

Whiner.

Frank ran down off the ship and talked to Officer Con Reilly before the cops drove away.

"What did you say to Con?" I asked when Frank got back.

"I told him that he should check Brian's house for the missing jewelry," Frank said. "He said he'd call when they did."

I smiled. "They're going to put Brian away for a long time when they find it," I said. But Frank didn't smile back. "What's wrong?" I asked.

"There's something not right about this," he said. "I know Brian's a jerk, but I can't believe that he followed the show around all summer, robbing jewelry stores as he went. I mean, what's the point? And if he *had* stolen all that jewelry, why did he need to be on the show?"

"Maybe the loot got mixed in with the fake treasure," I guessed, "and he needed to get on the show to win it back. I did find the necklace among the fakes, after all."

"But how would *that* have happened?" wondered Frank.

"You're not saying you think he's *innocent*, are you?" I asked. I couldn't believe that my brother seemed to be sticking up for Brian Conrad!

"I don't know," he said. "Something's just not right."

"You're overthinking it, bro," I told him. "Why not just enjoy the party—and the fact that Brian's on his way to jail?"

Frank nodded and grinned, just a little. "That is pretty sweet," he admitted.

By that time, most of the show's production crew had gathered on the ship along with the contestants. The PAs were moving through the crowd, debriefing people, telling them about the next challenge, and organizing a very late lunch. Others were prepping the ship for that evening's Treasure Island shoot.

Marlene Krall, Pedro Alvarado, and Miles Stillman stood near the ship's back rail as Samantha Olson bounded up the steps to the bridge. The designer was all smiles. Even though our case seemed over, Frank and I couldn't help but listen in.

"It looks like the cops got the saboteur, Ms.

Krall," Samantha Olson said. "Someone told me that kid they took away has been following the show around all summer."

"If he was willing to put a razor in his prop sword," Pedro Alvarado said, "I bet he would be willing to sabotage the show in other ways, too."

"He probably even killed Clay," Miles Stillman suggested, "and maybe Samantha's dad, too." Samantha winced at that.

"I'm sure the police will sort all that out," Marlene Krall said. "It's about time they found the troublemaker." She looked very relieved. "Maybe now we can film the show without any further incidents."

"Great," said Stillman. "I hope so. You're not paying me enough to reshoot a lot of scenes." He grinned at Krall, but I got the feeling he wasn't kidding.

Krall and her PAs rounded up the remaining contestants. They divided us into five groups for that evening's Treasure Island event. Initially they split us by last name—which meant Frank and I were with Kenya Krugman, as well as a couple of other people we didn't know.

Then, on camera, we drew marked stones from a jar for position within the group. Wouldn't you know it? Frank and I came out dead last, with

Kenya right in front of us. We were going to have a lot of ground to make up if we wanted to win this contest.

After that we went to the costume tent to freshen up and wait until the crew was ready to shoot on Treasure Island.

As we relaxed and drank bottled water, Frank's cell phone rang.

"Aunt Trudy checking up?" I asked.

He checked the ID and shook his head. "Con Reilly," he said, and then answered it. A minute later he clicked the phone shut.

"You won't believe this," he said, "but the police *didn't* find the jewels at Brian's house."

Frank was right: I couldn't believe it. "Not even the one he stole from me?"

"Nope," Frank replied. "What's worse, Brian has an airtight alibi for two of those jewelry store robberies. He wasn't anywhere near the show during those dates—he was here in Bayport."

"In a holding cell, no doubt," I muttered.

"Con didn't say," Frank said, "but I told you something didn't feel right."

I shook my head. "That means this case isn't over," I said. "Whoever stole those jewels is still out there and could still be making trouble for the show."

"Assuming they're the same person," Frank pointed out.

"It'd be a pretty big coincidence if they weren't," I replied. "Rats!" I had really been hoping that we could just relax and enjoy the competition. "Who do you think it could be?"

"Loot like that could cover the loss on a big prize win," Frank observed.

"You mean for Alvarado," I said. "Yeah. Some stolen jewelry could make up for that two million he's promised to pay. That kind of bling could also keep a struggling show afloat without a sponsor."

"You think Krall is that ruthless?" asked Frank.

"Bro, we fell off the rigging and she put it on the evening news," I said. "I think she'd do anything to keep *Buccaneers* going. You heard what she said about needing this season for rerun syndication."

"We can't rule out the contestants, either," Frank said. "They're all in this for the money too. So's everybody else connected with the show."

"Everyone but us," I reminded him.

"We're forgetting something," Frank said.

"What?" I asked.

"If the thief is still with the show," he said, "why did the robberies suddenly stop?"

"Maybe the criminal had enough loot already," I suggested. "Or maybe they were close to getting caught and decided to lay low for a while."

"But then why sabotage the show? Why kill Clayton Folwell? And what about Greg Olson? Was that part of their plan, or was his death an actual accident?"

I shook my head. "Bro, we've got a lot of pieces to this puzzle, but I'm still not seeing the big picture."

"Me neither," Frank admitted.

"I guess we'll just have to keep playing the game and see what happens," I said.

A couple of minutes later Paula rounded everybody up and herded us onto the ship for one of Stillman's on-camera speeches. The sun was setting when we came out of the costume tent, and the pirate ship and fake island looked pretty spectacular in the semidarkness. Big floodlights had been put up, and the combination of sets and shadows made it all look like a real pirate movie.

"Cool," Frank whispered.

Captain Stillman wasn't aboard the *Buccaneers* ship this time; he was standing in a skiff, tied up on the "shore" of Treasure Island.

"Avast, me hardies!" he bellowed. "Are you ready to hunt for loot on Treasure Island?"

"Aye, Captain!" we all responded, as usual. The lengthening shadows made the contestants and crew appear more like real pirates, too. Everyone looked dark and mysterious, especially Stillman.

"Crew," Stillman said to the dressed-up PAs aboard the ship with us, "hand out the treasure maps."

The crew pulled out a bunch of old-looking pieces of parchment and handed one to each contestant. Each paper was a map of Treasure Island, with a bunch of *X*s marked here and there, but no other instructions.

"As is buccaneer tradition," Stillman explained, "X marks the spot for treasure. You'll be noticing, though, that there are many of you and *not* so many treasures. That's where the competition comes in.

"The first sixteen buccaneers who find a treasure chest will continue on to the next test. The rest will join the other losers in Davy Jones's locker!" Stillman laughed his usual piratical laugh. Personally I was getting pretty tired of it, but I guess the TV audience was still eating it up.

"Now," he continued, "unfortunately we only have one skiff to get to Treasure Island, and I've already taken it. The rest of you will have to climb down the old-fashioned pirate way."

He directed our attention to five ropes, each

at least fifteen yards long, stretching from the big ship down to the island.

"You've already drawn for your position on the ropes," he said. "Now get in line and, at my signal, begin climbing."

"Aye, Captain," we all responded.

"Do you think we could slide down?" I whispered to Frank.

"Maybe," he said, "if we covered our hands. Kenya's in front of us, though."

Kenya Krugman, decked out in her fake dreadlocks and purple and gold pirate costume, had already taken her place at the rail, right above the first rope line.

"Kenya," I whispered. "We're thinking of sliding down the rope. Do you want to go with us?"

Kenya didn't respond. She didn't even turn around. "Game face," I whispered to Frank.

He nodded. "I guess we'll just have to wait and see what she does," he said.

"Is everyone ready?" Miles Stillman bellowed. I think we'd have heard him from the smaller ship even if they didn't have a wireless mic pinned to his costume.

"Aye, Captain!" we all replied.

Stillman pulled the fake pirate pistol from his

belt and pointed it up into the air. "On my mark, then!" he called.

The people who were first in line leaned toward the ropes.

BLAM!

The first contestants grabbed their lines and zipped over the side. Apparently Kenya had heard our suggestion, because when her turn came, she looped a greasy blue kerchief over the rope and quickly began sliding down.

Frank and I pulled the sleeves of our shirts over our hands and went after her. Our shirts slid okay, but Kenya was moving like lightning. It was almost like she'd known what was coming and prepared that kerchief in advance. Frank and I were only about halfway there when Kenya hit the beach.

She stumbled a little when she landed, shoved her hands into the sand and braced herself, and then got up and ran toward the center of the fake island.

SNAP!

For a moment I thought Stillman had fired his pistol again.

The sound was different, though, and the next second I realized why: Not five feet ahead of me, the rope had snapped—just like on the rigging challenge.

Without warning, Frank and I were suddenly falling into the cold, dark waters of Barmet Bay.

FRANK

13. Treasure Frenzy

I couldn't see what had happened ahead of Joe. All I knew was that I heard a strange snapping sound, and suddenly the rope gave way and the two of us were falling.

SPLASH!

We hit the water hard and sank under. I kicked my way to the surface. The play of sunset and floodlights on the water disoriented me, and for a moment I didn't know where I was.

Joe came up beside me. "Swim for the island!" he said. "We're not out of the contest yet!"

We swam as fast as we could and soon reached the fake island. Unfortunately the edge of the barge stood several feet above the waterline.

"What happened to the rope?" I asked as we grabbed hold of the side.

"It just broke after Kenya hit the beach," Joe said.

"Did she cut it?" I asked.

"I don't see how she could have," he said. "She wasn't anywhere near it when it broke. She just stooped down on the beach to get her balance and then took off running."

We pulled ourselves up, and I noticed that two of the other ropes had broken as well. The contestants who'd been using them were floundering in the water behind us. Those still waiting to slide down had been forced to join the remaining two lines. It seemed unlikely that three ropes would break by accident.

Joe noticed it too. "Do you think this is some kind of stunt the show orchestrated?" he asked as we crawled up onto the sand.

I looked over to Captain Stillman, standing in the skiff near the back end of the fake island. He looked pretty confused.

"I don't think so," I said. Just then my hand found something beneath the top layer of the sand: a trip wire. "Check this out," I said. I gave it a tug and something under the sand gave a mechanical click. "I think this trip wire has something to do with the ropes breaking."

"More sabotage!" Joe hissed. "Kenya could have set it off when she landed."

"But did she do it deliberately?" I wondered.

We looked at Kenya and the other contestants already scampering around the shadowy island, pushing one another out of the way, looking for treasure. We were about the fifteenth to land, and we were already well behind in the hunt. "Let's ask her," Joe said.

"No," I said. "If we stop now, we could be eliminated."

"Then what do you suggest?" Joe asked.

"Let's work together," I said, pulling out my map. "Two can dig faster than one. At least one of us needs to stay in the game if we're going to have a chance to catch the murderer."

The island barge was a veritable maze of rocks, bushes, fake palm trees, and of course sand. Even using the maps they'd given us, it was tricky to pinpoint where the treasures might be.

"Let's try by that squarish rock," I suggested.

As we ran to the rock, one of the other contestants pulled a small treasure chest out of the sand and held it above her head. "Found one!" she shouted jubilantly. Opening it, she cried, "A plasma TV!"

"Arrgh! Congratulations!" Stillman shouted from his skiff.

"Fifteen prizes left," Joe muttered.

"And fifteen chances to move on to the next round," I added.

We dropped down next to the squarish rock and started digging with our hands. "Too bad we didn't bring a shovel from the ship," Joe grumbled.

"It looks like Kenya was thinking ahead—again," I said. "Look!" I pointed at Kenya Krugman as she darted through the shadows. She pushed two other contestants aside and ran toward a bunch of fake coconut palms. As she went, she pulled a small ax out from under her billowing shirt.

"Where'd she get that?" Joe said.

"She must have hidden it in her costume before she slid down the rope," I replied.

"Is that legal?" he asked.

Just then another contestant shouted, "Got one!"

We looked up and saw him on top of a coconut tree on the far side of the barge. In his hand he held a big fake coconut, split in half. Inside there was a small treasure chest. He opened it and cried, "The car! I got the car!"

I looked from that cluster of fake palms to the stand where Kenya stood. One of the trees in her group had a set of floodlights on it. She picked the tree next to the electrified one and began chopping.

"Frank," Joe said, consulting the map, "there's

no *X* near that stand of trees. There shouldn't be any treasure there. What's she doing?"

"Look out!" I cried as the tree Kenya was chopping fell toward us.

Sparks flew as the tree pulled down the light stand in the tree next to it. Joe and I dodged to either side, barely getting out of the way in time. Half of the island plunged into darkness. Aboard the ship, Marlene Krall screamed with frustration. "Get some lights over there!" she said. "Keep filming! Keep going!"

Kenya scampered forward, dreadlocks flying, and began scooping up the coconuts from the fallen tree. None of the coconuts looked large enough to hide one of the game's tiny treasure chests. Several of the coconuts had split open, though, and something glittered inside.

"Has she gone crazy?" Joe asked.

"Crazy like a fox!" I said. The whole case started to come together in my mind. "She's the saboteur!" I cried. "The stolen jewels must be hidden in those coconuts! Grab her!"

The fake tree had fallen between us, and Joe was closer to the saboteur. While I climbed past the plastic fronds and the sparking wires, Joe jumped up. He caught the criminal by the toe as she ran past. Both of them tumbled to the sand.

"Wait a minute!" Joe said, getting a good look at her for the first time. "You're not—" But before he could finish the sentence, she rolled over and clouted him on the side of the head with a coconut.

Joe went down like a sack of potatoes. The saboteur sprang to her feet and ran toward the skiff where Miles Stillman stood, looking confused.

I skidded to a stop next to my brother. "Are you all right?" I asked.

"I'll be fine," he grunted. "Don't let her get away!"

As I ran, she reached the skiff.

Stillman started to say something, but before he could react, she hit him in the head with a coconut too. The actor collapsed into the boat. The pirate jumped in and pulled a tarp off the rear of the skiff, revealing a powerful outboard motor.

She started the engine and then went to the captain's motionless body. I think she was planning to push him overboard, but just then she saw me running full speed toward her.

Instead of pushing Stillman over, the saboteur untied the rope that held the boat to the fake island.

I'd nearly reached the skiff by the time she finished. I ran forward, ready to pounce, but I'd forgotten about her ax.

She reached back and threw it at me.

I hurled myself flat on the sand and the ax sailed over my head—barely.

By the time I got up, the skiff had already pulled away from the barge.

The saboteur gunned the engine, but she hadn't reeled in the rope. It trailed behind the boat like a long tail.

I knew I couldn't catch the skiff—but I could definitely catch that line.

Springing with all my might, I dived into the water and grabbed the rope, hoping to slow the skiff down.

14.
Keelhauled

I did a double-take as Frank throw himself into the water, trying to catch the runaway skiff. For a moment I thought I was hallucinating. Jumping after a speeding boat is the kind of thing *I* usually do, not my brainy older brother.

Everybody associated with the TV show was running around like chickens with their heads cut off. None of them had any idea of what was going on, or what to do about it. I knew what to do; I followed Frank into the drink.

I caught hold of the tail end of the rope just as the pirate girl gunned the skiff's engine.

The boat shot forward, dragging me and Frank behind it like wakeboarders without any board. I pulled myself up the rope close enough to talk to Frank as we bounced between waves.

"She's . . . not . . . Kenya!" I gasped as we bobbed up and down.

"I . . . know!" Frank replied. I would have asked him how he'd figured it out—he hadn't gotten a good look at her, like I had—but both of us were kind of busy right then.

The pirate ran the skiff at full throttle, pulling us out toward the open sea. We tried to pull ourselves up the rope, but the water pressure was too intense.

Even so, our added weight was slowing the pirate down considerably. With luck, dragging us might give the police time to catch up to her.

"Uh-oh!" Frank said.

"What?" I asked in between sprays of salt water.

"She's . . . spotted us!"

Sure enough, the crook had noticed the weight we added to the line. She pulled Stillman's pirate sword from the scabbard and, with one swift move, cut the rope free from the stern of the boat.

Frank and I bobbed to a stop and the skiff roared off into the night.

"Rats!" I cried, slamming the water with my fist. "She's getting away! And she's got the loot, too!"

Frank shook his head in frustration. "She had this whole thing set up ahead of time. I bet she planned her escape even before she figured out exactly where the stolen jewels were. That's why she rigged that outboard motor into the skiff."

"So she guessed the jewels were on the island because that's where Folwell had been working the day before he died," I said.

"Yeah," said Frank. "Folwell must have knocked open a coconut while working on the lights in that tree. That ruby-studded necklace was inside—the one she stole back from you yesterday."

"She must have figured out the location today, after filming started," I said. "Otherwise she'd have gotten the jewels last night, after everyone went home."

"Exactly," Frank agreed. "I bet she's been looking for them ever since the robberies ended."

"Which happened when the real thief died," I said.

"Right when the sabotage began," Frank added. "We probably would have put that together sooner if we hadn't been caught up in the game."

"And gotten sidetracked by Brian," I admitted. Funny how a few minutes with nothing to do but tread water can give you a new perspective.

"Well, Brian was a pretty conspicuous suspect," Frank said.

"The *most* conspicuous," I agreed. "So she knew

the jewels were on one of the *Buccaneers* sets, because she knew who stole them. But since she didn't steal them herself, she didn't know where they were hidden."

"Right," Frank said. "The sabotage was just a way to slow the show down while she searched. She didn't want anyone else to stumble across the loot accidentally—but Folwell did. His finding that necklace forced her hand."

"Too bad for him," I said. "She's been a step ahead of us, but we almost had her! I guess it's up to Con Reilly and company to catch her now."

Frank squinted into the darkness. "We may get another chance yet," he said. "She's coming back!"

Sure enough, the skiff had turned and was headed straight for us.

"She knows I recognized her, despite the disguise," I said.

Frank nodded. "She can't afford to leave us alive."

My eyes went wide as the boat zoomed in. "She's going to run us down!"

"She's going to *try*," Frank said. While we'd talked, he'd been reeling in the cut rope from the skiff. Now he held it looped in one hand, like a rodeo cowboy.

"Do you have a plan?" I asked.

"You bet," he said. "When the boat stops, climb aboard as quickly as you can."

"You're sure you can get it to stop?"

"Positive," he said.

"How about we get out of the way first?" I asked.

Frank didn't have time to reply—the boat was nearly on top of us. We dove under as the skiff zoomed in.

The boat was fast, but it sat high in the water. We didn't even have to go down six feet to avoid it. As it sped past, my brother and I bobbed to the surface again.

"It didn't stop," I noted.

"I missed," said Frank, coiling the rope again. "Give me another chance."

"I'll give you as many chances as she gives us," I said. "Let's hope she didn't stash a gun aboard that skiff."

"Yeah, let's hope."

The skiff came in on us again, bearing down full speed. The pirate had her sword in hand again, ready to slice us in half.

"Dive!" I said as the pirate reeled back. She swiped with the sword. Frank and I went under.

The boat roared overhead once more. In the dark water I couldn't see Frank, but I hoped he'd avoided the sword. A cold chill ran through my gut at the thought that maybe he hadn't.

In the next instant the engine of the skiff sputtered to a stop. Good old Frank! Somehow he'd used the severed rope to foul the boat's propeller.

I shot to the surface, aiming for the silhouette of the boat overhead.

I burst up out of the water and grabbed the side of the skiff, taking the pirate completely by surprise. She'd been leaning over the engine, trying to see why it stopped. When the boat lurched, she lost her grip on the sword and it tumbled into the water. She turned at me, enraged, as I pulled myself over the side.

She lunged at me, and I could see how, in the darkness, her pirate disguise had fooled everyone into thinking she was Kenya Krugman. I hoped that the real Kenya was okay, but only for a moment. Then I was struggling for my life against the pirate girl.

She swung a coconut at me. I blocked it with my forearm. The blow hurt, but not as much as it would have if she'd beaned me. The coconut popped open and a shiny piece of jewelry fell out, right on top of Miles Stillman.

The buccaneer captain was still lying in the bottom of the boat. She hadn't had time to toss him out yet. As the fake Kenya and I struggled, Stillman started to wake up.

Unfortunately the actor got himself tangled around my legs. The fake Kenya sneered and came at me, looking to hit me with another coconut.

I ducked, put my head in her gut, and heaved to my feet.

The pirate girl flew over my shoulder and into the air. She sailed out of the boat and hit the water with an awkward squawk and a huge splash.

"Nice job!" Frank said from the opposite side of the skiff.

I went over and helped him aboard. In the bottom of the boat, Miles Stillman moaned groggily.

"Let's get that saboteur back into the ship," said my brother.

I nodded. The two of us went to the other side of the boat and pulled her out of the bay. She'd hit the water hard and was pretty out of it. She didn't give us any trouble. Frank took the sash from around his waist and used it to tie her hands behind her back.

Miles Stillman sat up. "What happened?" he asked blearily.

Frank and I smiled at him.

"You just captured the *Buccaneers* saboteur!" I said.

FRANK

15.
Pirate Legacy

"I did?" Stillman asked.

"Yup," Joe said. My brother looked really pleased with himself, and I couldn't blame him. Letting Stillman take credit for the capture would keep us—and ATAC—out of the spotlight.

"I don't hardly remember," Stillman said.

"She hit you in the head," I told him. "You're probably just a little disoriented."

The saboteur sat in the front of the boat and fumed. "You didn't catch me, you idiot!" she said to Stillman. "These two did!"

"Well, we might have had *something* to do with it," I admitted.

"But you helped," Joe assured Stillman. "And we're happy to let you take the credit."

Stillman blinked and peered into the darkness, looking straight at the saboteur. "Samantha Olson?" he asked.

"Yup," I said. "She's been behind all the trouble at *Buccaneers*. She sabotaged the games, and she killed Clayton Folwell."

"I almost didn't recognize her in that costume," Stillman said. "But why? Why did she do all this? Why'd she cause all this trouble?"

In answer, Joe picked up one of the coconuts that Olson had gathered while she was pretending to be Kenya Krugman. He put his hands on either side of the shell, twisted a little, and cracked it open. Inside was a piece of glittering jewelry. Even under the dim light of the rising moon, all of us could tell that the piece was valuable.

"She's a jewel thief?" Stillman asked.

"No," I told him. "Her *father* was. I guess his *Buccaneers* salary just wasn't cutting it."

"Neither is mine," said Stillman. "I don't think anybody on the show is happy, except for Marlene. A show this big, you'd think they could afford to pay people better."

"Maybe Greg Olson was a jewel thief before he joined the show, or maybe he took it up during filming," Joe said. "We don't know. But he apparently used the show as cover for his crimes, moving from city to city with the *Buccaneers* ship, robbing jewelry stores as he went. That's what started the rumor of a 'crime wave' following the show."

"And it's why the robberies *stopped* a couple of months ago, after Greg Olson died," I said. "Sam knew about her father's robberies, didn't you?"

She stared daggers at me and didn't answer.

"Unfortunately," I continued, "you didn't know where he'd hidden the jewels. And you didn't find out before he accidentally drowned." I leaned over the stern of the skiff and began to untangle the rope from the propeller.

"Her father was the prop and set creator for the show," Joe explained. "He had access to everything, so she had a lot of places to look for the loot. She needed time to do it, and she didn't want anyone else finding the stash before she did. Isn't that right, Samantha?"

"Shut up," Samantha Olson said. "You don't know anything."

"Wrong!" I replied. "We know pretty much *everything*, don't we, Joe? It took us a while to figure it all out, but now we've got all the pieces of the puzzle."

"Clayton Folwell accidentally found some of the loot while he was rigging lights to that palm tree on the island," Joe said. "We know he figured out your dad's connection with the series of jewel robberies. When Frank and I first met Folwell, he threw something into the bay. At the time we thought it was a rock, but now I'm pretty sure it was a coconut—one of the fake ones your dad hid the jewels in. Folwell also let it slip that he'd discovered the secret and found the proof. He was pretty drunk at the time, and—unfortunately for him—probably blabbed to other people as well."

Joe looked at Samantha, but she didn't say anything.

"Folwell hid the proof—one of the necklaces he'd found—in among the show's fake treasure," I continued the story. "Maybe he didn't want to try to take it off the set with so much security hanging around. In any case, he probably thought it would be inconspicuous among all the costume jewelry—and he was right. Who'd have thought to look for the real goods among fakes? But Folwell was drunk and didn't realize that stash of treasure was to be used the next day."

"He did move the fakes, though, just in case," Joe said. "Remember how the treasure went missing and Folwell said he'd moved it? After Folwell died, Paula turned up the stash and used it in the treasure diving event. That's how I found a *real* necklace during the dive."

My brother looked at Samantha again; she stared coldly back at him. "*You* stole that necklace from me while I was tussling with Brian Conrad," Joe said. "You recognized it as part of your father's loot. A little detective work must have led you to Folwell before then."

"Using Brian Conrad as a decoy was a slick move," I said, "and it threw us off the scent for a while." I finished unsnagging the skiff's propeller and started the engine again, then angled the small boat back toward shore.

"But Brian had no reason to kill Folwell, and he wasn't smart enough to rewire the electric eel maze or set up the other accidents," Joe went on. "You, on the other hand, had both the talent and—as the show's designer—the keys to the power room. You also had the skill to rig the ropes to break and cause the other accidents by remote control, all while you set up convenient alibis."

"It's funny that the first event that went off without a hitch was the diving event you'd personally guaranteed," I told Samantha. "You didn't want to make yourself look bad, I guess."

"You think you're so smart!" Samantha hissed.

"We outsmarted *you*," Joe retorted.

"You were lucky," she snarled. "That's all. My dad worked hard for that loot. We needed it! He wanted to send me back to school so I could get a real engineering degree instead of being bossed around by idiots like Marlene Krall."

"Well, now you can work on that degree in prison," I said.

"Though I doubt that you'll ever get out to use it," Joe added.

As we approached the dock, Miles Stillman rubbed his head where Samantha had hit him. "That's a lot to take in," he said. "I never would have suspected Samantha. How did I catch her? I forget."

"She was trying to run me over with the boat," I said. "Even though you were groggy, you helped Joe toss her overboard and rescue me."

Stillman smiled. "That sounds like me, all right," he said. "I wish I remembered it better!"

"They're lying, you old ham!" Samantha said. "You didn't do anything."

Miles Stillman puffed out his chest. "Who do you think the police will believe, young lady," he asked, "a murderer like you, or me and these boys?"

"I want my lawyer," Samantha said. She clammed up until we reached the shore.

The police were waiting. They'd been called after we took off in the skiff, and after Paula found the real Kenya Krugman tied up in the rear of the costume tent. We were more than happy to hand Samantha over to Con Reilly and his officers.

Just as Joe and I had planned, all the media attention focused on Miles Stillman's supposed heroics. Stillman was happy to take the spotlight. Marlene Krall was happy as well, though not *too* happy.

"I think she's afraid Miles will ask for a raise," I told Joe.

"Wouldn't you if you were him?" Joe replied.

I laughed. "ATAC doesn't give raises."

"But they do give us cool equipment from time to time," Joe added. "Speaking of which, I think we should use our cool ATAC bikes to get out of here."

"You don't want to stick around?" I asked. "I'm sure they'll have to redo the last round of the contest. One of us could still be named the top buccaneer."

"I've had enough pirates to last a lifetime," Joe said. "I'd rather use the rest of my vacation doing *fun* things."

"But what about the treasure?" I asked. "It'd be pretty sweet if one of us won that top prize."

"Have you forgotten?" Joe asked. "No one has *ever* won the top prize in *Buccaneers*."

I laughed. "And if the sponsor has his way, no one ever will." Then I slapped my head. "Oh, no!"

"What is it?"

"We captured the real saboteur," I said. "You know what that that means, don't you?"

Joe sighed. "Yeah," he grumbled. "It means that they'll have to let Brian out of jail—unfortunately."

"Too bad," I agreed. "They could have cut down Bayport's crime rate by keeping him there *permanently*."

NEW STORY! FULL-COLOR GRAPHIC NOVEL
THE HARDY BOYS
#9
TO DIE OR NOT TO DIE?
based on the series by Franklin W. Dixon
UNDERCOVER BROTHERS
Scott LOBDELL • Paulo HENRIQUE
PAPERCUTZ

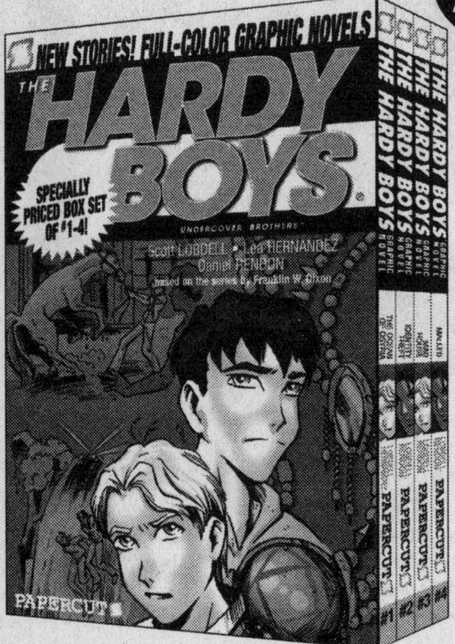
NEW STORIES! FULL-COLOR GRAPHIC NOVELS
THE HARDY BOYS
SPECIALLY PRICED BOX SET OF #1-4!
UNDERCOVER BROTHERS
Scott LOBDELL • Lea HERNANDEZ
Daniel RENDON
based on the series by Franklin W. Dixon
PAPERCUTZ
THE HARDY BOYS GRAPHIC NOVEL
#1
#2
#3
#4